"Have you ev[er]...

Gillian sounded breathy even to her own ears.

"I'm not blind. Of course I have." Alex fingered a strand of hair near her cheek. "You dazzle a man."

He made her heart quicken. Emotion filling her, she sighed as he slipped a hand behind her neck. "This is crazy, isn't it?"

"Why?" Alex believed they couldn't keep ignoring this. He wanted to hold her, feel her soft contours. She kept staring at him with eyes that appeared even more seductive than usual. He'd always thought she was one of the most beautiful women he'd ever seen.

He'd touched her dozens of other times, but something was different this time. Why? They were supposed to be good buddies, nothing else. They'd never had a future together. Yet he wanted her. He wanted her as he'd wanted no other woman. "Tell me what you want, Gillian. What you really want...."

Dear Reader,

Silhouette Books publishes many stars in romance fiction, but now we want to make *you* a star! Tell us in 500 words or less how Silhouette makes love come alive for you. Look inside for details of our "Silhouette Makes You A Star" contest—you could win a luxurious weekend in New York!

Reader favorite Gina Wilkins's love comes alive year after year with over sixty Harlequin and Silhouette romances to her credit. Though her first two manuscripts were rejected, she pursued her goal of becoming a writer. And she has this advice to offer to aspiring authors: "First, read everything you can, not just from the romance genre. Study pacing and characterization," Gina says. "Then, forget everything you've read and create something that is your own. Never imitate." Gina's *Bachelor Cop Finally Caught?* is available this month. When a small-town reporter is guilty of loving the police chief from afar and then tries to make a quick getaway, will the busy chief be too busy with the law to notice love?

And don't miss these great romances from Special Edition. In Sherryl Woods's *Courting the Enemy*, a widow who refused to sell her ranch to a longtime archrival has a different plan when it comes to her heart. *Tall, Dark and Difficult* is the only way to describe the handsome former test pilot hero of Patricia Coughlin's latest novel. When Marsh Bravo is reunited with his love and discovers the child he never knew, *The Marriage Agreement* by Christine Rimmer is the only solution! *Her Hand-Picked Family* by Jennifer Mikels is what the heroine discovers when her search for her long-lost sister leads to a few lessons in love. And sparks fly when her mysterious new lover turns out to be her new boss in Jean Brashear's *Millionaire in Disguise!*

Enjoy this month's lineup. And don't forget to look inside for exciting details of the "Silhouette Makes You A Star" contest.

Best,

Karen Taylor Richman,
Senior Editor

Please address questions and book requests to:
Silhouette Reader Service
U.S.: 3010 Walden Ave., P.O. Box 1325, Buffalo, NY 14269
Canadian: P.O. Box 609, Fort Erie, Ont. L2A 5X3

Her Hand-Picked Family

JENNIFER MIKELS

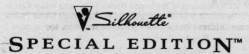

SPECIAL EDITION™

Published by Silhouette Books

America's Publisher of Contemporary Romance

To Laurie Feigenbaum, my agent, a great big thanks

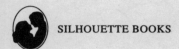 SILHOUETTE BOOKS

ISBN 0-373-24415-0

HER HAND-PICKED FAMILY

Visit Silhouette at www.eHarlequin.com

Printed in U.S.A.

Books by Jennifer Mikels

JENNIFER MIKELS

is from Chicago, Illinois, but resides now in Phoenix, Arizona, with her husband, two sons and a shepherd-collie. She enjoys reading, sports, antiques, yard sales and long walks. Though she's done technical writing in public relations, she loves writing romances and happy endings.

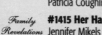
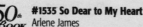

Prologue

"Gillian, don't surprise him. You told me he doesn't like surprises."

Gillian Quinn smiled and shifted the phone receiver from one ear to the other. Her sister never forgot anything. "Rachel, he'll help me, even if I don't call first." She tugged on one kinky curl of her recent permanent. After weeks of having others mess with her hair, as a model at a hairstylists' convention—even dying her naturally red strands a bright magenta—she'd chosen a shoulder-length corkscrewed style that meant "no fuss, no bother."

"I know what a good friend he is to you, but—"

"Don't worry so." Gillian looked at the digital clock she hadn't packed yet. "I promise I'll call him before I leave." Next stop was supposed to be Hawaii and a new job. But a recent revelation about her family had altered her plans. She needed to make another stop first, in Arizona.

"Are you sure Alex will go with you to look for her?"

Gillian had no doubt at all. A professor of archaeology at a northern Arizona university, Alex Hunter was reliable, practical, steady. Whenever she'd needed someone to lean on, he'd been there for her. Whenever she had to talk to someone, to ramble on to about a decision, to weather a broken heart, she'd called him. He was her best friend, the one person besides her sister and brother who would never let her down. "Yes, I'm sure."

She longed to see him and his daughter, Shelby, again. She worried about them. After his divorce she'd flown from her home in New Mexico to Colorado to see them. She hadn't known if he'd needed a comforting shoulder. He'd assured her that he hadn't. His marriage had been over long before.

Since then, four months ago actually, he and his daughter had moved to Arizona. Life couldn't be easy for a single parent, she thought, and she kept hoping Alex would find someone with whom to share his life.

Chapter One

"Should I call the police?" Alex Hunter's land-lady yelled to him.

Alex paused beside his Bronco and watched her rush from the front door of her redbrick bungalow. Widowed Loretta Yabanski had added a second floor to her home to provide her with additional income. Seconds ago Alex had arrived at the house to the sight of her waving her arms to get his attention. She was an ample-figured woman with a dimpled smile and light brown hair threaded with gray.

As his father emerged from the passenger's side of the vehicle, Loretta spoke to him. She'd had an eye for him ever since Joe had moved in to Alex's apartment nearly a month ago. "Joe, what should I do?"

"Loretta, calm down," he said in the same stern tone Alex assumed he'd used to issue orders during a good portion of his years of military service. A tall man, he stood ramrod straight. Immaculate in his appearance, Joe had kept his gray hair cropped military short. His square-shaped face bore a few deep lines, but he carried his age well. "What's the problem?"

"A strange woman is in the backyard, sitting on one of your daughter's swings, Alex. I never saw her before."

The red-and-white swing set had been hell to move, but when Alex had rented the apartment from Loretta, he'd looked for a way to give his daughter a sense of permanency and had asked Loretta if she'd mind the swing set in her yard temporarily. The woman had proved to be an angel of a landlady, baking cookies, supplying them with casseroles, even baby-sitting.

Right now she looked worried, and Joe wasn't helping to calm her. "What kind of adult sits on a kid's swing?" he bellowed and whipped his cell phone from where it was hooked on his belt.

"Wait," Alex insisted before his father dialed 911.

His father's ice-blue eyes darted to him with disapproval. Alex's caution had been a note of contention between them all through his youth. *Make a decision, boy. Snap to it.* He'd heard those words often enough. *The enemy could have you surrounded by the time you decide.*

Life was not about military maneuvers and strategy, Alex had wanted to say. As a kid he'd kept his mouth shut to stay out of trouble. As an adult he stayed silent to keep peace. "Let's hear what she's doing there first," he suggested.

"She's trespassing," Joe barked. "That's what she's doing."

Loretta nodded agreeably, staring up at Joe as if his words were golden. "She's dressed odd in a neon-green baseball cap and jeans with daisies at the hem and green shoelaces in her sneakers and—"

"Like one of those hippies," Joe said.

Alex had to remind him. "That was in the sixties and seventies, Joe." For Alex to refer to him as dad never entered either man's mind. "It's probably Gillian. Does she have bright-red hair?" Alex asked. He knew only one woman who owned neon-green shoelaces and a matching baseball cap.

"He knows her?" he heard Loretta question behind him as he led the way along the walkway at the side of the house to the backyard gate.

"College friend," Joe said simply.

"But she's so different," Loretta murmured.

Probably he and Gillian seemed like an unlikely pair, but after dancing around each other through weeks in an archaeology class and barely tolerating each other, a field trip to Utah had changed everything.

He'd witnessed her dedication, her discipline, her willingness to work hard at uncovering prehistoric Native American wooden bows while other students' enthusiasm had waned beneath the dry and hot weather, and he'd no longer seen her as the impulsive, flighty girl who sat beside him in class. Like every other male in the class, he'd already noticed the way sunshine shone on hair the color of copper, the willowy body, the long slender legs in the snug jeans.

Respect for the hard work each had willingly endured, and mutual pleasure over the discovery, had drawn them closer while they'd been on that dig. Before they'd returned to New Mexico, they'd become friends.

He studied her now, let his gaze travel over her slender back. Just the sight of her brightened his mood. Sitting on the red swing, she was staring dreamily at the distant mountains in the northern Arizona town.

As he approached, a twig snapped under his foot. With her red hair swirling in the late-August wind, she twisted the swing chains and swiveled a look over her shoulder. Her hair flew away from her oval-shaped face. A glow colored her peaches-and-cream complexion, and her green eyes sparkled. "Oh, Alex."

Arms out, Alex braced himself as Gillian flew at him for a hug, and he rocked back on his heels to stare at an all-too-familiar grin. He hadn't realized how much he'd missed her until that moment.

"Oh, I've missed you," she said, laughing when he crushed her to him.

With her so close, he felt as if she'd never been away, yet it was the first time he'd seen her in eight months, since before he'd moved to Arizona. An unmistakable warmth heated him. That wasn't unexpected. He reasoned that being close to any woman might have caused the same reaction. By choice, because he'd had enough family problems to deal with, he'd been without a woman for a while. Hands cupping her upper arms, he studied her. A seriousness darkened green eyes that could haunt a man's mind. "Come on in," he suggested.

"Where's Shelby?" She kept her arm around his waist and walked beside him toward the back stairs. "I'm dying to see her."

"She went to a friend's house after preschool. She has a few more days. Then kindergarten starts."

"Does she like—?" Her steps faltered. "Oh, Joe. Hi!" She rushed to him. "It's so good to see you." She tossed her arms around his neck. "You look wonderful," she said, drawing back.

Always reserved, he returned an awkward hug, then glanced Loretta's way.

"Hi, I'm Gillian Quinn," she said before Alex managed an introduction.

Loretta, all smiles now, said, "I almost called the police about an intruder."

Her eyes friendly, Gillian set a hand on the woman's shoulder. "Well, I'm glad you didn't."

"Yes, so am I."

"I'm sorry if I scared you." She returned to Alex's side and slid her arm around his back again.

"Alex, you wait a minute." Loretta scurried ahead of them up the back steps to the first-floor porch.

"She's getting food," Joe guessed.

"Probably," Alex agreed. "Loretta believes food is good for everything. Stub your toe, she'll give you a brownie. Have a problem, she'll bake bread."

"How sweet. I'm surprised you two aren't

blimps.'' Her hand flattened against Alex's midsection. Instinctively it tensed at the unexpected contact. He really had been without a woman for too long. ''It's good to know you're not getting soft,'' she teased. ''Still do the nightly torture session with the rowing machine?''

''Still do.''

At the bottom step she twisted around to look at Joe. ''In a phone conversation, Alex mentioned that you two were dating.''

''Yes, we are.''

When Gillian turned away, not for the first time Alex smelled lilacs, a fragrance that always made him think of her.

''Here you are.'' Loretta's voice sang. She stood before them with a casserole dish in her hands. Alex prayed it wasn't tuna casserole. ''A welcoming dinner.''

''That's nice of you, Loretta,'' said Joe, who'd passed them on the steps to take the dish from her. Since Joe looked pleased, Alex assumed it was lasagna, his father's favorite. ''Why don't we go to a movie, Loretta?'' Joe asked.

''I'd love to.''

''Good. I'll be back in less than five minutes,'' he assured her, and took the stairs with swift efficiency.

Loretta beamed. ''Wasn't that nice of him?''

Puzzling, Alex decided. Joe hadn't mentioned plans for a night out with Loretta.

''That was nice,'' Gillian said, beside him.

Alex climbed with her to the second-floor porch. ''What was?''

''That he left us alone, gave us privacy.''

His apartment door flew open, and Joe hurried down the stairs, passing them.

Gillian laughed at his quick ''bye'' and entered the white kitchen. ''Obviously, he thought I'd come for more than a visit.''

Alex didn't have the heart to argue with her. Open, friendly, she tended to think the best of everyone, but Joe had never shown concern for his feelings. ''Is there a reason?''

''I did call,'' she said, instead of answering. She dropped an oversize denim shoulder bag to the floor near the small chrome and Formica table. ''I hope this isn't a bad time.''

He sent her a you've-got-to-be-kidding look. Stopping beside a cork bulletin board near the phone, he looped his keys on a hook. The blinking light on the answering machine caught his eye. In passing, he hit the playback button.

''Hi, it's me, your very best friend Gillian Quinn,'' the female voice sang. ''I'll see you later today.''

''Told you,'' Gillian piped in over her own voice. ''A short and sweet message, to the point just like you prefer.'' She flashed a hundred-watt smile at him, one of those smiles that guaranteed he'd do whatever she wanted. ''Say 'I'm happy to see you, Gillian.'''

''That goes without saying. It's great to have you here.'' The message wasn't important. Why she'd left him one, instead of materializing unexpectedly the way she always did, bothered him.

He was frowning, thinking too much, Gillian

guessed. He certainly looked as wonderful as ever. Tall with broad shoulders, he carried an air of confidence and intelligence. Sun-kissed brown hair, a strong jaw, ice-blue eyes and an ample share of muscles completed the package, one that tended to make his female students drool. "I'm glad to be here." She stepped near for another hug, hadn't realized how much she'd needed his steadiness, his logic in her life until that moment. He would keep her from doing something rash. He'd keep her from acting impulsively, jumping to conclusions.

"But something is wrong."

She'd thought she'd veiled her anxiousness behind her best smile. "Why do you think there's something?"

"Because you called instead of just popping in." He was silent for a second. "And you sound distressed."

She was hopeless. *You wear your emotions for everyone to see.* That's what she'd been told often enough. *You're too passionate about everything you do.* But she didn't know how to do things halfheartedly. "I'm not worried."

"I didn't say worried. You sound anxious. Why are you?"

Too easily he zeroed in on her moods. "Couldn't I have wanted to see you?"

"Nothing is ever that simple with you."

"Oh, puleeze." He was the complicated one, a deep thinker, an introspective man. "You're the one who can't do anything without a list of reasons. She really didn't consider that a bad trait but loved to tease him about his need for checklists and schedules.

"Want something to drink?" He opened the refrigerator and held up a can of her favorite soda. In typical Alex fashion, he backed off from asking more questions. It was one of his finest traits, knowing exactly when to prod and when to back off.

"Yes." Shelves in a cupboard had been stocked with meticulous care, cans lined up, labels facing forward. "Are the cans alphabetized?"

"Cute. They're organized." With her nod, he yanked at the tab on the can and offered it to her. "Beans are there," he said, pointing to cans. "Corn, peas."

Gillian laughed. "They're alphabetized."

He grinned, letting her have the last word.

The cans weren't alphabetized, but everything was orderly, categorized. There was a time when she'd been less than impressed at his methodical manner, thought he was too rigid, too persnickety. Now she viewed those qualities as endearing. She remembered the exact moment when her opinion of him had changed. She'd been working side by side with him since daybreak at the Utah dig. By sunset everyone had been hot and dirty and tired. Though he never smiled at her, she also never heard him complain.

They finished brushing dirt away from several wooden bows, then in celebration, they'd collapsed in each other's arms. She'd noticed then how rock solid he'd felt beneath her hands. She remembered raising her face to his and wondering about a kiss. But as if they'd both been aware, they'd pulled back.

They hadn't kissed, but from that moment on, a friendship had begun.

He was so sensible, so serious, so responsible. He was also one of the most loyal, caring and intelligent men she knew. There had been times when she regretted that they'd never transcended the step beyond friendship and become lovers. But in retrospect, she supposed this was best.

"Now tell me what you're going to talk me into."

"When did I ever do that?"

"Too many times to count. Like half a decade ago. You talked me into a harrowing experience of riding the rapids."

He protested too much. She believed he'd really wanted to go, or it would have taken her more than a minute to convince him that he would enjoy himself. "You wanted to go."

A vague smile touched the corners of his lips as he lounged against the kitchen counter. "Of course I didn't."

Questioningly she inclined her head. "Then why did you go?"

"Because I wasn't going to leave you alone with that guide."

"Which one?"

"You know which one. Mr. Macho with the tan and bulging muscles. The guy that leered at you all the time."

She had the good grace not to smile. "Alex, were you jealous?" she teased because she was certain he'd never had a lustful thought about her.

"I was praying my lunch, beef jerky and dried apricots, stayed in my stomach."

She recalled now that he had kept a white-knuckled grip on the edge of the boat.

"So what kind of help do you need?"

Ever since her sister, Rachel, had found their mother's diary, she'd struggled with the secrets unveiled. "I need to find someone."

"And that person lives here? In Arizona?"

"Near a university. I've checked for the name Selton. That's the only information I really have. A name. Lenore Selton." She went on. "I checked Phoenix and Tucson telephone directories, but there's no one listed by that name."

"So you're guessing that she's living here, in Flagstaff?"

"Possibly."

"I thought you had a job in Hawaii. How can you take time to do this?"

"I don't have to be there right away."

"Finding this person is important to you?" he asked while reaching into a cupboard for a can of coffee.

"More than you know." She moved to the doorway, stared at the living room with its wall-to-wall furniture. They were definitely cramped here.

"Tight quarters, huh?" he quipped, stating the obvious.

Because being less than honest never occurred to her, she nodded. "Yes." She looked away from a kitchen bulletin board adorned with Shelby's drawings to see him measuring coffee grounds into the basket of the black coffeemaker. She knew how much he liked quiet time with his books. Being crowded must be difficult for him.

"Besides this room and the living room, there are two small bedrooms and a closet-size room for Shelby."

She asked the obvious question. "It's difficult now that Joe's here?"

"We're sardines in a can."

She assumed he'd thought of a solution. When she'd talked to him two weeks ago, he'd mentioned his father's visit. Retired, Joe had had a heart bypass and was staying with him. Now he was having a vision problem. She doubted any of this was easy for a man who was used to being in control. "What's the plan?" she asked, returning to the table.

"I'm doing the obvious. I'm looking for a house. I only took this apartment temporarily."

She recalled how thrilled he'd been that he'd be able to finally settle somewhere with his daughter.

"After they offered tenure, we rushed here. I packed a moving truck and drove here with Shelby and took the first decent place that was available. At that time my biggest concern was finding a nanny for her."

Always, his daughter came first. "I wish I'd been available to help back then."

"Hey, you weren't even in the country. You were in Japan. That was when you had that air courier's job."

She knew he was right, but it still seemed unfair

that he hadn't been able to depend on her. "You were fortunate to find Loretta. She seems nice."

"She thought you were a mental institute escapee."

Gillian laughed, taking no offense. "I did notice how she kept frowning as she stared at my outfit."

"It's not conservative enough for Loretta's tastes."

Or his, she thought, but wearing jeans and a gray polo shirt, he didn't look as conservative as he used to in his button-down shirts.

Passing by her, he flicked a finger at the hair sticking out from the back opening of her cap. "I have to get dinner started before Shelby comes home."

There was something in his eyes. She ruled out a problem with Shelby. He'd have already confided in her. Perhaps Joe's illnesses were rousing concern in him. "Why don't you heat the lasagna?"

He held a package of thawed ground beef. "Joe would have fits if we ate it without him. He loves Loretta's lasagna."

Gillian arched a brow. "Is the way to his heart through his stomach?"

"Who knows?" He offered her a bag of tortilla chips. "Here's a hold-me-over."

"Is he sweet on her, too?"

"He wouldn't admit it." He set a salsa jar before her. "But sure he is. Want to shred cheese?" he asked while opening the refrigerator.

"Anything. If it means getting it done faster. What are we eating then?"

"Tacos." Over the refrigerator door, he grinned at

her. "Did you only get one bag of peanuts on the airplane? Usually you can charm three or four bags from the flight attendant or other passengers."

"I was more tired than hungry."

For a few minutes they worked side by side in silence. Alex admitted that it felt good but strange to have a woman beside him doing something so domestic. He'd gotten used to being alone. That probably wasn't best for Shelby or him, but it seemed easier. He didn't want to see his daughter get hurt. If he kept his life simple and didn't complicate it with relationships that might not last, she'd be better off.

"Now what?" With a plop, she dropped the shredder in the soapy dishwater. "Want me to set the table?" She was already opening and closing cabinets. "Dishes are…?"

"Up there," he answered, pointing to an oak cabinet to the left of him. He looked out the window. Streetlights illuminated the dark street. He wanted to ask her now what was wrong, but he heard a car door, knew the quiet wouldn't last.

"Daddy, Daddy, I'm home," Shelby yelled loudly enough to be heard in the next house.

"Who would have guessed," Alex said in a wry tone when Gillian swung around. She smiled—and took his breath away. Why? He frowned as he faced the door. He'd seen her smile thousands of times, so why that reaction this time?

Chapter Two

Her dark hair gleaming beneath the overhead lights, Shelby barreled in. Steps from Gillian she came to an abrupt halt, then flew at Gillian's opened arms. "Gillian. Gillian, I missed you."

The baby fat cheeks were gone, and her hair was longer now. Gillian squeezed her gently. How wonderful it was to hold her. She drew in a breath, reveling in the sweet scent of her. "Not as much as I missed you." Little arms held her neck in a stranglehold. Shelby looked like her mother. At five, she was delicate looking, with raven-colored hair and deep blue eyes. A decade from now she'd be stunning.

"I missed you lots," she said. "Are you staying?" She swung a look at Alex. "Is she, Daddy? Are you...?"

Alex smiled. "Shelby, take a breath."

She giggled, an indication that he'd needed to stop her rambling questions often. "What are we eating?"

"Tacos."

"Ohh, tacos. I love tacos." She grinned up at Gillian. "Daddy said he'd make them tonight. Do you like tacos?"

She hasn't changed, Gillian mused as Shelby rambled about the frog she lost, about starting kindergarten, about a new friend.

Tightly she gripped Gillian's hand with her small one. "Do you want to see the gorilla? The one you sent. It's in my room."

Gillian laughed, lifted her up to eye level and sent Alex an apologetic look for leaving him to do all the work. "Mind if I desert you?"

"That's all right. While you're there, I'll get your suitcases."

Gillian stilled with Shelby in her arms and whirled back to him. "Alex, I can't stay here."

"Sure you can. You can take my bedroom."

Adamantly she shook her head. "Absolutely not. I'm not pushing anyone out of his bed."

"You won't be. Tomorrow you can have Joe's room. He's going to a reunion for a few days, so he'll be gone. Your timing was perfect."

"Are you sure?" she asked, but felt less concerned that she was causing any inconvenience.

Shelby angled her head to put her face in front of hers. "You can sleep in my room tonight. We can have a sleepover. Can't we, Daddy?"

"If you do, you'll have to share the bed with her stuffed animals."

Gillian touched the top of Shelby's head. "That's no hardship. I had my own collection until I was seventeen."

Shelby's eyes rounded. "You did!" Gillian could tell that she was definitely impressed. "Don't you have it anymore?"

"No. I was going somewhere and couldn't expect my sister to keep it for me."

"Daddy will keep mine forever. Won't you, Daddy?"

By the way he beamed at her, Gillian imagined he would. "Come on, Shelby. *We'll* get my suitcases. I'm traveling light."

Alex swung around. "I'll do it."

She was already on her way to the door with his daughter. "No, you're busy. And there's not much."

Alex gave up any notion of arguing with her. She was already gone from the room. She was like a whirlwind, whisking in and out of his life for the past five years. He always was thrilled to see her and exhausted by the time she left.

Palming a head of lettuce, he thought about the last time she'd visited. She'd been headed to Alaska to see an Iditarod race. During a phone call several weeks later, she'd said she was in Japan, then phoned again with news that she was catching a flight to San Francisco to model in a hairstylist's convention. She'd always been willing to try anything, a woman with a streak of wanderlust, who rushed everywhere as if she might miss something.

At the sound of feminine laughter, he stopped chopping the lettuce to see Shelby maneuvering a carryall through the doorway. A step behind her, Gillian entered with a garment bag draped over one arm, a carryall hooked to her shoulder and a suitcase in each hand.

"Give me those," Alex insisted. "You call that traveling light?"

Gillian had thought so. Though she kept the garment bag, she relinquished the suitcases to him and trailed Shelby. Because of the trip to Hawaii, she'd sold her car, a ten-year-old MG in canary yellow. She'd hated letting it go, mainly because it had been such a great buy, and she'd gotten it dirt cheap from a guy who lived and breathed the ocean and wanted money for a new surfboard.

"That's Daddy's room." Shelby pointed to her left.

The walls were white, the bedspread hunter-green, gray and white, and the furniture, cherrywood. Shelves in a corner of the room above an antique, roll-top desk displayed his collection of antique books, salt-glaze stoneware and several African tribal masks.

Her gaze shifted from a mystery novel on the bedside table to the open door of his closet. Shirts and pants were arranged by color, all facing in the same direction. "Alex, you're so neat." Aware of him scowling behind her, she stifled a grin and followed Shelby. Actually she admired his orderliness. She'd always wished she'd mastered that trait. But despite her best efforts to keep things in an organized fashion, she found things easier when she surrounded herself with clutter.

"This is my room," Shelby announced with pride, garnering Gillian's attention.

It was small with two twin beds. Youthful and feminine, it was messed just enough to look comfortable. The bedspreads were a soft-blue color with a print of Looney Tunes characters. Shams and matching bed skirts in pale-blue and white stripes complemented them. Her stuffed animal collection with a giant-size Sylvester the Cat and a Tweety Bird occupied a corner of the room and the top of the one bed. A small bookcase held dozens of books and several keepsakes. Scattered around in the center of the room were dolls and doll clothes.

Shelby stood close. "Do you like it?"

"I love it." Like a prized possession, the child-size gorilla that she'd sent was sitting in the center of a stuffed-animal collection.

Alex left the luggage, saying nothing about the disorder. Because he was such a neat freak, Gillian decided he deserved a pat on the back for good parenting skills. For a few more minutes she visited with Shelby, learned the names of Shelby's dolls while she scrounged through a cosmetic bag filled with her costume jewelry. "I'm going to help your daddy now," she told Shelby, leaving her sitting in the middle of the bed, admiring a strand of black beads.

Steps from the kitchen the melodious strains of Beethoven's Fifth Symphony reached her. Until that moment she'd forgotten how much Alex liked to cook. He'd spend hours in the kitchen, slicing, dicing, sautéeing, and in between, he'd direct an imaginary orchestra with whatever kitchen utensil was in his hands. She waited for the crescendo and the final notes. With panache, he finished conducting on an upswing. "Do you still have everyone convinced that you're the stuffy professor, maestro?" she asked from the doorway.

Startled, he swung around and pointed the spatula at her. "I do if you don't give me away."

She couldn't help smiling, aware he didn't really care what other people thought. "Would I tell them that you lead orchestras while you cook and sing opera in the shower?"

He pulled a face. "Forget you learned that."

During one visit she'd stood outside the bathroom door and listened to his rendition of *La Traviata.*

"Here." He held out a spoon. She viewed the action as evasive strategy to avoid more discussion about his impersonation of Pavarotti. "Stir the meat." And while you do, tell me what brought you here."

"This is really complicated." She realized she had never considered what she'd do if he didn't help. She'd simply assumed that he would. "I'm trying to find—a brother or sister."

He pivoted away from an open drawer. "What are you talking about?" His brows veed. "You don't know where Sean or Rachel are?"

"Yes, I know where they are. There's another one." She held up a hand before he asked another question. "Rachel found out that we have another sibling. We don't know if it's a brother or sister."

He looked dumbfounded. She and Rachel and their brother, Sean, had passed through a myriad of emotions since learning their father had been with another woman, had learned that she'd gotten pregnant. "It's such a mess, Alex," she said, revealing her own disbelief. "Rachel went back to Maine where we used to live, to the house where we'd all grown up. Well, actually the house belonged to Kane Riley.

"He's her new husband. I told you that they'd gotten married. It wasn't a big affair, but—" She angled her body toward the stove as he squeezed behind her to reach a box of taco shells. "My sister looked absolutely breathtaking and elated." Her voice softened. He was close, so close the heat of his breath caressed her face. She looked up, found his gaze on her. With another man, she'd believe she was about to be kissed.

"You said they have a baby?"

She was slow to answer. "Yes. Kane's niece," she said, sure now that she'd imagined his look. "It's a long story, but Rachel was friends with his sister, and she died when she had the baby. Now Rachel and Kane and the baby are a family."

Alex presented his back to her and frowned while he slit open the cellophane-wrapped shells. A minute ago he'd been close enough to see specks of brown in her green eyes. A minute ago he'd had to drag his gaze away from her mouth. "Sit down," he urged. He switched off the burner and gestured toward the table.

"This is all so hard to believe." Gillian set the spoon in a spoon holder by the stove. "Even for us.

A fisherman, Charlie Greer owned the house after we left and never bothered to check the attic. Neither had Kane, after he inherited the house from Charlie.'' She paused. ''You're confused.''

He felt a small pounding at his temple. ''Muddled.''

''Okay. What's important is that my sister, Rachel, found one of our mother's diaries in a trunk in the attic.''

Alex straddled a chair near her.

''Rachel learned that a woman named Lenore Selton had an affair with our father decades ago and had become pregnant.''

Alex hunched forward. She'd said that so matter-of-factly, he'd be a fool to believe she was that untouched by such a revelation.

''It was a shocker for all of us,'' she admitted. ''According to the diary, he had the affair when my mother was ill. She had a nervous breakdown. Actually I guess it was worse than that. She was institutionalized for nearly a year after a miscarriage.'' She frowned with him. ''It must have been a terrible time for both of them.''

''Do you remember it?''

''Oh, no.'' As if lost in thought for a long moment, she stared at the colorful curtains with their brown, orange and yellow teapots pattern. ''I wasn't born yet. But Rachel remembered our mother being ill. And she helped Dad take care of our brother. Sean was only five then. But there's more. While Rachel was in Maine, at the house, she found an adoption paper.''

"Adoption—who's adopted?"

In a small show of nerves, she bounded to a stand and snatched up the bag of tortilla chips. "We thought I was."

He watched the crease between her brows deepen. That possibility couldn't have been easy for her.

"Let me explain. My mother's diary indicated that she had planned to adopt Lenore's baby, which is why we wondered if one of us was that child."

Slowly he nodded. What she wasn't saying came through clearly. "Okay. But you don't believe that now?"

"No. Rachel read in one of the diaries that Lenore changed her mind, so none of us could be that child." She nibbled on a chip.

"That's who you want to find?"

"Yes. We know that Lenore left Maine for Arizona back then to join her sister, Edith Selton. To find Edith is one of the reasons for my visit."

"Go on."

"Edith was a teacher like our father and Lenore, and she taught at an Arizona university."

"Have you…?"

"I checked with the other universities. She didn't teach there." Gillian crossed to the window. "I want to find Lenore, meet the woman my father's supposed to have been with. And the child Lenore had."

Alex said nothing for a moment. As she offered her back to him, he stood and stepped close behind her. "Look at me," he insisted. Slowly she faced him. She didn't need to say a word. Reading her doubts made him push. "Why don't you believe that your father had an affair?"

"You always need reasons, don't you?"

Her question bothered him. Did she see him as too analytical, too rigid in his thinking because he needed a purpose for everything that was done? At one time she had thought he was boring, persnickety, too stodgy.

"I know what you're doing." She delivered a smile that looked strained to him. "And it's really sweet of you."

She was losing him.

"But I'm not letting emotions lead me. Honest." In what he viewed as a stall, she made much about dipping a chip in the salsa sauce.

"You've thought this through, then?"

"Yes." She sighed heavily with an admittance. "You're right. I'm not sure my father had an affair with Lenore Selton. We only have Mama's take on this. From the first day Rachel told me all of this, I've wondered if this was something our mother had made up."

"Because she was ill?"

"Yes. She was so grief-stricken after her miscarriage. She wrote that she'd wanted nothing to do with our father during those months afterward. Their marriage was practically nonexistent for almost a year. She wasn't a wife, companion or lover to him. It's then that our father supposedly had the affair." It hurt to say the words. "He was wonderful, Alex. A warm, loving, gentle man, an honest man. I wish you'd met him. He was the most wonderful father in the world.''

''Why would your mother write that if it wasn't true?''

''I can only guess. My father and Lenore were both teachers. I don't doubt they might have been friends. Maybe he learned she was pregnant. You have to remember how my mother was then. She was mourning the loss of a baby. What if, to help her, he suggested that Lenore let them adopt her baby? None of what we've learned verifies that Lenore was pregnant with his child.''

Doubt shadowed him. ''You said only your mother was adopting the child, Gillian.'' He believed in facing realities head-on. It was something he'd learned to do at the end of his marriage. ''That would probably mean he was the biological father.''

''This makes no sense to me. He had no contact with the baby. If it was his, he would have. He was too responsible not to keep in touch.'' She shook her head. ''The more I learn, the more questions I have. If all this is true, then I need to know what Lenore was like.''

''Meeting her might be painful, Gillian.''

''It might be. But I'm going to do that, anyway. I need proof that all of this happened.''

''Daddy!'' Shelby rushed in, rubbing her stomach. ''Can we eat now?''

Gillian smiled, grateful for a breather from her family problem. ''Sounds as if someone is really hungry,'' she said with more brightness than she felt. But she wanted to simply enjoy being with Shelby and Alex. For one night she didn't want to think more about a revelation that had rocked her family.

"It's almost ready." Alex set a plate with the lettuce and diced tomatoes on the table. "Tell Gillian what you want to be for Halloween," he said, leading conversation down a lighter path now that Shelby was with them.

Gillian played along, and looked heavenward. "Let me guess. Do you want to be a princess? Or a ballerina?"

"A taco," Alex teased while filling a bowl with the meat mixture.

Shelby reacted predictably. "Daddee! That's not what I want to be."

He stood by Shelby's chair as she scooted onto it, then began filling a taco shell with meat, lettuce and cheese for her.

"I wanted to be a polar bear. They're my very favorite animals, but we looked and looked and looked for a polar bear costume and can't find one. But I did find a cow one." She bit into her taco. "What will you be, Gillian?"

"I might not be here, Shelby." Head bent, Gillian spread the meat mixture, cheese and lettuce onto a taco shell. "I have a job to go to."

Alex paused in pouring red punch in a glass decorated with cartoon characters. Despite her whimsical side, her eyes conveyed a steadiness of spirit that had always appealed to him. "What about that job?"

"I told you. Several months ago an old acquaintance Reed Turney called and asked if I wanted a job with his air taxi service."

Protectiveness rose within him. In his opinion Reed Turney sounded like a sky cowboy, a thrill seeker. He thought the guy probably was smooth, used to women thinking he was special.

"Earth to Alex."

He snapped his attention back to her. "What?"

"This is so good," she said with a gesture toward the taco in her hand. "I could inhale this."

He set Shelby's drink in front of her, then took a seat. He'd guess Gillian had been running non-stop all day. "Did you have anything to eat today?"

She shrugged. "Are you going to lecture me about skipping meals?"

He spooned refried beans onto his plate. "I know that would be a waste of time. So this guy Turney offered you the job and you snapped it up." He had to ask. "Why? Are you interested in him?" *Is he a lover?*

"We're friends."

Her answer didn't ease his mind. Sometimes he followed the swing of her hips, the casual loose-limbed stride, felt his gut tighten. And he wondered about her. It would be difficult for any man to be friends with her and never fantasize. She was lovely, bright, smart. Most of all she had a knack for making a person feel good.

Her voice sang. "You're zoning out again."

"Sorry."

"What is wrong with you?"

Damned if he knew. "Tired, I guess."

"Troubled, I'd say." She placed a hand over his. It was slender, soft. She had long fingers, could have played the piano. She'd chosen the flute instead, she'd told him, because she'd heard an Irish song "The Kerry Dance" and had loved it so much that she'd wanted to learn to play it. She'd performed it for him once. It was lilting, romantic, a song about lovers. He gave his head a mental shake. What the hell was his problem tonight? "You always wanted to go to Hawaii."

"I was thrilled to get the opportunity to go there. But Reed didn't need me for a few months, and I got the modeling job in San Francisco. Now there was an experience. They were doing hair in every color conceivable. One woman walked around with rainbow-colored hair for two days." Her smile faded. "That was about the time Rachel uncovered everything. I called Reed and told him I needed time."

"I don't understand. Don't you have to make arrangements to move your things, or aren't you expecting to stay in Hawaii for long?"

"I have everything."

His eyes narrowed with incredulity. "In three bags?"

"A neighbor kept my books and CDs for me. I gave the beige sofa to another neighbor, and the wrought-iron stools for the breakfast bar went to my landlord. I sold the rest of the furnishings." To her, the job offer in Hawaii had sounded like a chance to live in paradise. A life on the islands would be blissful, exciting. "Come when you're ready, he said during our last phone conversation."

Gillian stretched for one of the napkins in a napkin holder on the counter. She didn't need to see Alex's face to know he was frowning. While she relished change of pace, spontaneity, flexibility in her life, he believed in more concrete plans. He couldn't conceive of dropping everything on the chance he might settle at some job on an island. "And since I don't have to be there for a while, I have time for family business."

"You're sure he isn't trying to get you there to—"

Now there was a question she never expected from him. "You sound Victorian."

"I'm careful," he insisted.

Beside him Shelby bounced in her seat. "You said you don't have to be there for a while. Then you might be here for Halloween."

"I might be." Gillian wanted to spend more time with Shelby, get to know the little girl better while she was around.

"We could go to that big, new store if you want to get a costume. Daddy, could we look for the polar bear costume there?"

Alex returned her smile. "Shelby, I told you," he said in a patient tone that indicated she'd been nagging him. "We'll go there."

Gillian loved being around them. So much love filled the room with one look shared.

"Why are you the one doing the search?" he asked, snapping her from her reverie.

She was surprised he'd brought conversation back to her problem. "With no family or work responsibilities, I was the logical one. Lenore Selton was only a name to us, but she has affected the lives of my whole family, if this is all true. And—'' She paused, looked for a delicate way to say her next words in front of Shelby. ''Then there's a person out there who might be family, Alex. We have to find that person.'' She set her napkin down and glanced at her wristwatch. ''Do you mind if I use your phone to call my sister?''

''Go ahead.'' He snatched a child's book from the counter. ''Shelby and I have to find a rabbit.''

Shelby finished the last bite of her taco. ''Uncle Lemmi is hiding in a cabbage patch,'' she added about the character in the book.

Alex urged her toward the door. ''Say hi for me.''

''I will.'' Gillian made the collect call and waited. She knew Alex liked her family. He'd met Rachel and Sean only once, had spent a few moments with them at the airport. But they were sensible, goal-oriented people, and he'd instantly felt comfortable around them. ''It's me,'' she said several seconds later in response to Rachel's hello.

''Did you surprise him?'' Rachel didn't sound as blissful as Gillian had expected.

''Yes, I did. But I want you to know that I didn't mean to. I called and left him a message, but he didn't get it. So he was surprised.'' She refrained from telling her worrywart sister that the landlady considered calling the police. ''It's really wonderful seeing Alex again. And Shelby.''

''Gillian, there's…there's something I need to tell you.''

She heard no smile in her sister's voice and instinctively tensed. ''About Lenore?''

''About her baby.''

Chapter Three

"Gillian, Lenore's baby died."

She leaned back in her chair. "What?"

"Mama wrote that Lenore's baby died. Since we talked the other day, I found a smaller journal only partially written in. I'm sorry. But Mama wrote that Lenore called. Wait. Let me read this to you." A moment passed. "Listen." Gillian heard her sister turning pages. "It's all so sad. Lenore called and told us about the baby—a girl—dying. Alan and I are heartbroken."

Gillian waited for her to read more, but she was silent. Something was wrong. All wrong. "That's all. That seems so—unfeeling. That's not like Mama."

Rachel was quiet for a long moment. "I felt the same way but didn't want to say anything to you. I thought I was imagining something. This all seems so sad. Why now? I'd finally accepted all that had happened, was looking forward to meeting the person that child had become.''

''And that's all Mama wrote?'' Gillian asked again.

''Yes. I guess that because of you, because she got pregnant with you about the same time that this was happening, she handled the news this way. Actually I hardly remember the time. Sean and I went to live with Aunt Cheryl for a while.''

Gillian could only imagine what their mother had gone through.

''I'm assuming they thought she'd do better without the stress of her children around her,'' Rachel said. ''When we did come home, she was there, and she was fine.''

Loretta's and Joe's voices behind her made Gillian look back. Since Rachel's news, she couldn't say what she was feeling. She shifted the phone to her other ear. ''I'll call next week,'' she promised Rachel after her sister said she'd call their brother with the latest news.

''I convinced Joe to stop at the little bakery on the corner,'' Loretta told her when Gillian turned to face them. ''They were getting ready to close, and we got the last of their éclairs. These are absolutely wonderful. And I thought they might sweeten Joe's mood,'' she said conspiratorially after Joe stepped out of the room. ''I don't believe he enjoyed the movie. He grumbled something about it being a 'chick flick.''' She sighed. ''Some men have no appreciation for romance. However, he does have many other fine qualities.''

''You like him a lot?'' Gillian asked, needing to think about something besides her sister's news.

''Yes, I believe I do. He's a little gruff, but then my Frankie was, too. But he had a soft center. I believe Joe might have one, too. It might be fun to find out. And what about you and Alex?''

''Me and...?'' Gillian scoffed at the idea. ''Hardly. We're just friends.'' She regretted those words. They made their relationship sound unimportant when actually she equated their closeness to the kind she had with her sister and brother. ''We're too different for that type of relationship.''

''Being different can sometimes make things interesting.''

Gillian paused in taking cups from a cabinet for coffee. ''He needs to find someone, but that isn't me,'' she assured Loretta. Alex needed home and hearth, wanted to provide his daughter with security. He needed a lasting relationship. She wanted no ties. She savored the unexpected, needed it as she needed air to breathe.

''Joe said you've been friends since college.''

''That's right.''

Loretta tipped her head in a questioning manner. ''Is that where Alex met Shelby's mother?''

''No. After graduation, which was a few months after I met him, Alex worked at a substitute teaching job in New Mexico and took part in several archaeological digs, then left for Colorado and continued his schooling to get his graduate degrees. That's where he met Nicole.''

"You liked archaeology, too?"

"Yes, but I got interested in other things. Like flying. I'm a pilot. Small planes," she added before Loretta assumed she flew a commercial plane. "Back then I was searching for myself. For the fun of it, I signed up for the class and met Alex. I didn't like him. In fact, we barely tolerated each other.''

Loretta tipped her head questioningly. "Oh, but why?"

Good question. What had been the problem between them? Neither of them had changed since those days. Sometimes he was still too serious, too careful. And she believed in having fun, sometimes lived on the edge.

"Something wonderful must have happened," Loretta said in a speculative tone as if reading Gillian's mind.

"We grew on each other," Gillian said for lack of a better explanation. But that barely skimmed the surface of her feelings for him. She trusted him. She would tell him things she wouldn't share with anyone, not even her sister or brother.

"Oh, yes, I understand that," Loretta replied, nodding agreeably. "I've been feeling the same with Joe."

What Loretta felt for Joe wasn't the same, but Gillian didn't bother to argue. Gillian thought the woman was delightful, and obviously falling in love with Alex's father.

"I wonder where he is. Oh, Alex," she said as he

appeared at the doorway. "Do you know where Joe is?"

"He's reading a book to Shelby."

"Oh, how wonderful." Loretta pushed back her chair. "I think I'll join him."

While she hurried out, Alex took the seat she'd vacated.

"She's smitten," Gillian said, enjoying the idea of love blooming between Joe and Loretta.

"What's happening with you matters more to me. Something is wrong."

She'd thought she'd masked her sad feelings since talking to Rachel.

The eyes staring at her were so intense. "Did your sister tell you something that upset you?"

"That I'm upset by her news might not make sense to you." She didn't even understand herself. Since Rachel's phone call, she felt a sense of loss. "Rachel learned that Lenore's baby died."

A deep crease formed between his brows. "All of a sudden she learned this?"

"Rachel found one more diary. I suppose she thought there wouldn't be more written about Lenore. But there was."

"I'm sorry," he said after a long moment as if he'd been letting his mind register what she'd said. "This changes your plans, doesn't it?"

"Not really. Though I won't look for our... sister." They knew now that it had been a sister. "Would you still ask around at the university about Edith? I'm hoping you can find someone who knew Edith or Lenore."

"What did Rachel say about this?"

"Rachel thought they might not want to talk about the past."

He caught her hand, held it in his larger, stronger one.

She felt the callused ridge on his palm from the rowing machine. "You see that on television programs all the time. I'd heard a story about a woman who denied she'd had a child." The idea of someone rejecting her own child appalled her. "I can't imagine."

"Why is it so hard to believe that a parent might reject a child?"

Gillian heard heat in his voice. Was he talking about himself? She wanted to ask him to explain. All he'd ever said was that they moved constantly, and his father was gone a lot, so they'd never been close.

The sound of small footsteps running drew their attention toward the doorway. Shelby burst in a second later. "Mrs. Yabanski said she brought dessert." Her blue eyes darted from the counter to the table. "Ohh, they look good," she said about the éclairs, not waiting for Alex's answer.

"Then you'd better have one," Gillian suggested. She was tired of talking, glad Shelby had wandered in. What more needed to be said?

At the sound of the ringing phone, she looked up. Alex stretched toward it, but it had already stopped ringing. On a shrug he lifted Shelby to his lap. Gillian smiled with them. They were so close, so connected. She'd been worried about them earlier, but they seemed all right.

"The phone call is for you, Alex," Joe announced from the doorway, the portable phone in his hand.

"It's a lady," Loretta whispered to Gillian as she joined them at the table.

"Ah, the next Mrs. Professor. You've been holding out on me, haven't you?" Gillian gibed. "There is someone special."

He set Shelby on a nearby chair, nudged a plate with an éclair toward her. "Enough," he returned on a laugh, shoving back his chair.

Amused, Gillian shared a smile with Joe as Alex left the room with the phone. "He needs to get married again," she said teasingly.

"Good idea," Joe responded, assuring her how he felt about that idea.

"He don't want a mommy. Me, either," Shelby insisted. She dropped the éclair in her hand onto the plate, slid off the chair and flounced out of the room.

"Joe?" Surprised and concerned, Gillian swung toward him for an explanation.

"I don't know," he said about her unasked question.

Gillian dropped the subject as Shelby returned, clinging to her daddy's back. Had she interrupted his phone call or had he bumped into her on the way back? For the moment neither Gillian, Loretta nor Joe mentioned Shelby's outburst. There had been too much pain in eyes so young when she'd made that statement. Because Alex was unaware of her reaction and Shelby had resumed eating her dessert with gusto, Gillian decided to say nothing. "These are the best éclairs I've ever had, Loretta."

As if determined to help normalize the moment, Loretta upped her bright tone. "This bakery is one of the finest. It has carrot cake to die for and wonderful cream puffs. And fudge brownies," she said pointedly, looking at Shelby. "Which are someone's favorite."

The little one had returned to her usual sunny disposition and smiled. "We should go there, Daddy. Grandpa likes brownies, too."

Beside her, Joe grinned, but concern remained in his eyes for his granddaughter.

"How long is the reunion?" Gillian asked to draw him into conversation.

"A weekend." He finally looked away from Shelby. "It will be good to see friends. A few of them live in California. I'll be visiting them first." His brows bunching, he kept his gaze on the dark liquid in his cup. "Seems best."

Gillian stifled a frown at the way father and son tiptoed around each other.

"I'll miss you," Loretta said.

As if she'd imagined his previous mood, pleasure touched his lined face now. Affectionately he closed his hand over Loretta's on her lap. "I'll call," he assured her. For a few more moments they made inconsequential conversation about the bakery, then Joe stood, drawing Loretta up with him. "Let's go for a walk."

When they headed for the door, Shelby disappeared in the other room to watch her favorite cartoon about a dog that played sleuth. Alex left, too, for a while.

Alone, humming a favorite Patsy Cline song, Gillian filled the sink with hot soapy water and began washing dishes. Because of her recent modeling job, her finances were in great shape. Though she might not need more than a few days to find Lenore, she could afford to stay for a few weeks.

"It must be a female thing. My daughter has a thing for bubble baths," Alex said on a laugh as he wandered back in and spotted her with hands plunged in bubbles of soap.

"Soapy water is soothing."

He sidled close. "You know you didn't have to do the dishes."

"Alex, don't try. I know you hate this chore. Did Shelby seem upset?" Now that they were alone, she mentioned the earlier incident with Shelby. "I'm sorry. That would be my fault for that Mrs. Professor comment."

"She seemed all right." He grabbed a dish towel and picked up a plate. "She played in the bath water and didn't even balk when she had to put on the green pajamas with the bugs."

She latched on to the humor in his voice. "She doesn't like those?"

"They'll do. But her favorite ones are pink and have a female superhero emblem on them."

"What do you think about what she said?" she asked, bringing them back to her original comment.

"I'm not surprised she reacted that way. She wants no part of a new mommy."

This made no sense to Gillian. Shelby had been a baby when Alex and Nicole had divorced. "Why?

She didn't even know Nicole.'' She watched water rush down the drain. ''This isn't about not wanting another woman to take her place, is it?''

Head bent, he dried a second plate. ''No, it has nothing to do with that.''

He might have said more but Shelby reentered. ''Will you read the book about the puppy and the horse?''

On the move, he scooped her into his arms. ''Grandpa read that earlier.''

''You could read it again.''

He kissed the tip of her nose. ''Guess so.'' Shelby giggled as he brought her around to his back for a piggyback ride. ''You know where we'll be,'' he said on the way out of the room.

Listening to Shelby's giggles, Gillian smiled after them. He really was more like his father than he realized. On the surface, especially in the classroom, he conveyed a formidable, no-nonsense demeanor. She'd listened to his lectures and saw the way he captivated an audience. But in both men a softness and a passion existed. Joe felt that for the military, for his country. Alex revealed it when he talked about ancient worlds and artifacts. But one thing ranked above all that—their love for Shelby.

While he was reading to her, Gillian showered, then slipped on a bright-orange sleeping shirt, and a navy silk wrap. She gathered the tie on her robe while she meandered into the hallway.

She stilled at Shelby's bedroom doorway to see Alex sitting on the edge of Shelby's bed. Softening his voice to a whisper, when she closed her eyes, he stopped in midsentence. He shut the book, then kissed her lightly. "She never makes it to the end of the story," he said in a low voice as he joined Gillian at the door.

"That's probably why she wants you to keep reading it." Gillian crossed to the other bed to remove the stuffed animals. With a Porky Pig in her arms, she looked around for a place to set it.

"On the floor," Alex suggested and stepped near, grabbing a polar bear and a skunk. He turned left, Gillian turned right. Hips brushed. Instinctively he reached out. It was a natural response because they nearly bumped into each other. But his hand touched her waist, and something slow and warm curled inside the pit of her stomach. She stared into his eyes and drew a deep breath. Several. Her heart beating hard, she nearly swayed into him. She could feel the heat of him, almost imagine his taste. Almost. This was not the way she always felt. This was not the way to feel with a friend.

"Told you we needed a bigger place." He spoke lightly, but his eyes flicked to her lips. Was he thinking about kissing her? "You can't turn around without running into something or someone," he added.

She was slow to answer. A longing had risen within her so swiftly she'd nearly rocked with it. "You have lots of problems lately."

"My share." Slowly, almost reluctantly, he turned away, grabbed the last stuffed animal from the bed, a lion. "That's the last of them. Do you need anything?"

"No, I'm fine." But she wasn't. There was a difference between them, and she didn't understand it.

In the dimly lit room, she'd seen something in his eyes, something unfamiliar. For years she'd made a point to remain detached, hadn't wanted to worry about anyone but herself. That had worked with everyone except Rachel and Sean, and Alex. That made sense. He was like a brother to her. Of course she'd feel something for him.

The problem was she did nothing halfheartedly. And no red-blooded woman wouldn't find him attractive, wouldn't react to him, she reasoned. Even in the past a touch, a brush of his body had sparked feminine response. But what she'd felt minutes ago meant nothing. Not really.

Keep telling yourself that, she railed at herself. Denial wasn't going to work. She'd stood near him, and excitement had stormed her. Her heart had beaten a touch faster, a pressure had risen within her chest. Those were not sisterly reactions. "I'll see you in the morning."

Gillian mustered up a smile.

At the door he stopped, looked back at her. She watched his eyes wander down from her eyes to her lips. "I'm glad you're here."

Nervously she brushed a strand of hair away from her cheek with the back of her hand. With more effort than she expected, she drew another deep, calming breath. "Me, too."

What the hell was that? Alex stood outside the bedroom and heaved a breath. Could he remember ever having been so aware of everything about her before?

His gut had tightened with her closeness, something had gnawed at him to take a deep, full taste of her. He'd placed a hand on her waist and had nearly let his fingers inch downward to the point of her hip.

He'd been without a woman too long, he mused. What other reason could there be for his reaction to her? This was Gillian, his buddy, his friend.

With slow steps he strolled toward his room. Before he drove himself crazy dissecting each moment, each touch, each look, he flicked on his VCR and a travelogue video about a trip along the Nile, then settled on the rowing machine. His legs bent, he rowed with a steady rhythm and tried to enjoy the scenery. It was useless.

He'd wanted to kiss her. Nearly five years ago he'd had that thought for the first time. At the dig in Utah he'd felt a jolt, the undeniable man-woman tug when he'd grabbed her in a celebration hug. What man wouldn't? She was slim, soft, smelled wonderful. She was a lovely looking woman with the kind of smile that made a person smile back, with eyes that fascinated. She'd made him laugh. She'd started talking and he'd felt as if no one else existed.

But he hadn't been a stupid man. He'd known physical attraction alone carried no lasting power and hadn't pursued her romantically. Now he had to wonder. He stopped rowing as a thought crept in. What if he'd made a mistake?

Not the hint of morning sunshine but the sight of two, huge brown buttons greeted Gillian when she opened her eyes. At some time this morning, Shelby had tucked the gorilla in bed beside her. "Morning, Mr. Snuggles," she said, recalling the name Shelby had said last night. She stretched, stared at the window and the gray predawn sky.

With the sound of male voices speaking in whispers in the other room, she peered in the direction of Shelby's bed, saw it was empty. Not oriented to her surroundings, it took a moment to locate the bedside digital clock in the room.

Gillian moaned. Were they all really up at six? They were all probably cheerful, too. A morning person Alex could have full conversations within minutes of getting out of bed. He even whistled before seven.

Rousing herself, she sat on the edge of the bed for a long moment. She needed a cup of coffee or a can of soda. She needed a jolt of caffeine. If she managed to get to the kitchen, to the coffeepot or the refrigerator without making contact with anyone, she might deliver a few sentences when one of them approached her.

"Gillian."

At the rap on the door, she winced.

"Are you decent? Can I come in?"

She stood, straightened the sleeping shirt's hemline. It definitely had shrunk during the last wash. Instead of skimming her knees, it ended about mid-thigh. "I'm okay." With her fingers she raked at tousled strands. She was a long way from okay. "Come in." The smell of coffee drifted in first. She eyed the cup in Alex's hand. He hadn't forgotten that she wasn't a good sport before her morning coffee.

"For you." He stopped beside her, offering the cup to her.

Thank goodness. Needing to get her bearings, she swallowed a hearty sip, then another. "This was nice. Thank you."

"I wanted you to know I was leaving."

"Leaving?" Her voice trailed off. Heat hummed through her with his slow, sweeping look down the wide-necked, orange nightshirt to her thighs. Somehow she resisted an urge to yank at the hem. Somehow she ignored the pressure in her chest.

"I'm going to drive Joe to the airport."

"Oh." Tongue-tied. Had she ever been tongue-tied before with him? Had he ever looked at her like that before?

He wasn't looking now, she noticed. Frowning, he'd turned away. "Shelby's watching cartoons. If you don't want to baby-sit, I'll stop by Loretta's and—"

"That's silly," she said to his back. "I'm here."

"Thanks." Even though he'd migrated toward the door, her mind wouldn't let go of the smell of his aftershave, a woodsy, masculine scent. "I'll be back in an hour."

Mentally Gillian groaned. None of this made sense. Why would she suddenly begin having these feelings for him? Why had he looked at her like that?

She grabbed jeans and wiggled into them, then tugged a gray pullover over her head. On the way to the kitchen, she fluffed her hair. She needed to stop making too much of the simplest things.

Perhaps because she was going through so much emotional upheaval, she was feeling more vulnerable. That made sense. Of course she would turn to the one person she trusted the most. Possibly, she was imagining feelings for him that didn't exist.

Chapter Four

In the kitchen Gillian refilled her coffee cup, and in between sips, wandered to the window. After an unseasonably warm day yesterday, a morning breeze carried a refreshing coolness. She wished she'd gone for her morning run. Though her days lacked any schedule, she did follow a few routines, and usually she worked through problems while she jogged.

"Are we going to eat now, Gillian?"

Gillian swallowed the coffee in her mouth, grateful she'd managed a few sips of cup number two before Shelby asked for breakfast. She prayed the youngster wouldn't want eggs. Breakfast was not her favorite meal.

"Can I have the cookie cereal?"

Bless you. "Sure you can." Though she would

personally prefer a chocolate brownie, Gillian willingly settled for the sugar-loaded cereal shaped like miniature chocolate chip cookies. While they ate, they watched a Tom and Jerry cartoon. She would have liked to question Shelby about her reaction yesterday, but she needed to gain her confidence first. They needed to spend time together.

She did just that, playing Old Maid, talking about favorite songs and colors and food. While Shelby went to the bathroom, Gillian asked Loretta to watch the little one. She jogged to the corner convenience store for bagels, but once inside, spotted a box of chocolate-covered doughnuts, a weakness of Alex's.

Though she didn't want to upset Shelby's routine, Gillian wondered if Alex would agree to let her take care of Shelby for a while and give Loretta days off. She really would like to get closer to the little girl.

Good as his word, within a few hours Alex returned. Feeling less unsettled, certain she had a handle on what she viewed as odd feelings about him, she gave him her best smile. "That didn't take long."

"Joe was flying with friends on a commuter plane. He didn't need me around. Thanks for watching Shelby."

"You don't have to thank me for that." Gillian shut off the spigot. "I love being with her. I'd like to spend more time, maybe play chauffeur today."

He reached for the dish towel. "She'd love it."

She heard the pride in his voice. Every time he looked at Shelby or talked about her, a message came through clearly. His daughter was everything to him. Though pleased now, she'd seen his frown when he'd mentioned Joe. She took the towel from him. "Let me do this. Have a cup of coffee," she urged, tempted to raise a hand to the frown line between his brows. How crazy this was. She had to get a grip on this, needed to be the friend he was used to having around. "Didn't it go well with Joe?"

"Before joining his buddies, he reminded me that I have three baby-sitters now." He poured coffee in one of those to-go mugs that the convenience store offered with a purchase. This one advertised the city's hockey team. "I can get out more."

Confused, she pivoted toward him. What was so bad about that? She waited while he refilled her cup. "Why do you sound as if you're gritting your teeth?"

"What does he care?" Irritation laced his voice. "I'm getting tired of everyone telling me that I need a mate." He sighed, shook his head in disgust. "Forget it. I'm acting—"

"Cranky?" she finished for him.

He cracked a halfhearted smile. "I guess so. Colleagues are inundating me with dates, hoping to find the 'perfect mate' for me."

"And you're not cooperating, are you?"

Now he grinned, a real one. "You know me well." As if in deep thought he stood for a moment, silent, then set down his cup. "I'll change the sheets on Joe's bed for you."

Gillian wrinkled her nose. Not for the first time he sneaked a look at his watch. He had somewhere to go, she assumed. "I can do that. If you treat me like a guest, I'll have to leave. Don't you have something to do?"

"A meeting in an hour."

"Then go. I know you wear a lot of hats." She imagined there were times when he felt ready to collapse beneath the weight of his responsibilities.

"Thanks."

Instead of moving, he scowled at the kitchen counter. What was out of place? she wondered. "Did I fold the dish towel wrong, not stack the napkins right?"

"You bought doughnuts. Do you know what's in one of these?" he asked, even as he opened the box and snatched up one.

"Thirty-three grams of fat," she read helpfully off the package.

"Plus things I can't even pronounce." Though he spoke in a disgruntled tone, there was a smile in his eyes when he paused beside her, placing a hand on her forearm. "Thanks. They're my favorite."

"I know," she barely managed. With his kiss on her cheek, heat swept through her. Again her heart quickened. Confused, she watched him turn away, cross to the door and close it behind him as if nothing had happened.

Alex relied on being rational. He knew she wasn't perfect. She left dripping wet washcloths hanging from the shower faucet. She ate some awful junk for breakfast. She dog-eared paperback books instead of using a bookmark. Whenever she washed dishes, she hummed or sang an old song, the same song, something about being crazy and feeling blue.

Crazy was how he was beginning to feel.

Before leaving, he'd deliberately moved near, kissed her cheek, tested himself. He was sure he would feel nothing, but not for the first time in the past twenty-four hours, he'd wanted to bring her against him, kiss her, really kiss her.

Ever since this morning, ever since he'd seen her in that thigh-length sleeping shirt, he'd wanted more, hadn't been able to stop thinking about her or forget how the cottony fabric had molded to her breasts and hips. She made him fantasize. She made him want.

And being around her suddenly wasn't so simple.

After making the bed, Gillian played one round of a memory game with Shelby. The little one's attention waned in fifteen minutes, and she left to play with her dolls.

At eleven-thirty, Gillian drove her to preschool. With time to herself she went to the shopping center. She treated herself to a salad lunch at a trendy California-type restaurant decorated in mauve and mint-green and accented with brass and greenery. Afterward, she went to a movie. The romantic comedy didn't help. Every time the couple kissed, she thought about Alex. She had no answer to why this was happening. No answer at all, she realized while driving to the preschool for Shelby.

Talkative as usual, the little girl shared her dislike for the cookies with prunes in them that one girl brought for snack time. "They looked like they had bugs in them. Yuk," she said, wrinkling up her nose.

Gillian held on to a straight face. "Terrible," she said in her most sympathetic voice.

"Will I be late for dance class?"

Gillian glanced at the clock on the dashboard. "Nope. I'll get you there on time."

They arrived five minutes before the three-thirty class. While Shelby dashed off in tap shoes to join the other girls, Gillian joined the parents sitting on chairs at the back of the huge room.

"They're doing so well, aren't they?" the young woman sitting beside Gillian said after several minutes of watching the girls go through their routines. Straight and shiny, the woman's brown hair swung with her movement as she looked back at the dance class. "My daughter is the third from the right."

Tall and thin like her mother, the little girl beamed at them while she did a shuffle-tap step.

"Which girl is yours?"

"Shelby. The petite, dark-haired one," she answered, not bothering to explain their relationship.

"Oh, she's so cute. Is she in ballet, too?"

Gillian recalled Shelby's pirouette earlier in the kitchen. "Yes."

"I love watching them. It's such fun to see them improve."

Gillian agreed. It was fun to sit like one of the mommies and watch the class. Mentally she smiled at the odd notion. That was definitely a Rachel thought. Her sister was the nurturing one.

"See you next week, Gillian," the woman said when the class ended.

Gillian nodded. "I'll see you." Only after she responded did she realize how easily the words had slipped out. She planned on coming, wanted to. She'd enjoyed herself, she realized as she crossed the large room to meet an exuberant Shelby.

She and Shelby stopped for ice cream, then browsed through stores for nearly an hour and a half. Exhausted after running from one store to the other to find a doll that sang, by the time they reached the apartment, Gillian had one thought. Sit.

She kicked off her shoes, and dropped to a chair in the living room while Shelby dashed to her room to change. Eyes closed, she visualized the ocean. Calm. Shimmering. Seagulls. Whitecaps.

"Gillian, someone's at the door."

Reluctantly she gave up the images as she heard soft rapping on the door. Though impulsive by nature, she wasn't idiotic and showed caution at appropriate times. "Thank you, Shelby." She waited until the little one headed back to her room, then wandered to the door and squinted through the peephole.

It revealed a tall, lean, studious-looking man with brown hair, a sharp-angled face, and a cleft in a rather pointed chin. He wasn't a handsome man but had kind, hazel eyes. "Who are you?" she asked through the door.

"I'm looking for Alex. I'm Grant. Grant—"

Gillian swung open the door before he finished saying his name. More than once, Alex had mentioned Grant to her. "He went to a meeting, Professor Denton. I'm Gillian Quinn.'' She stepped forward, offered her hand. ''Nice to meet you.''

''Gillian?'' His eyes brightened with warmth. ''Finally we meet. I've heard a lot about you.''

She could imagine what Alex had said. Often enough he good-naturedly shook his head in disbelief at her.

''I forgot that he had several departmental meetings all day.''

''Had,'' Alex said suddenly appearing behind him in the doorway. ''Two were canceled.''

Gillian assumed they'd want time alone and took a step to move away. ''I'll make a new pot of coffee.'' She also wondered what to do for dinner. It occurred to her that she, Alex and Shelby were the only ones here for the meal.

''No, no.'' Grant held up a hand, halting her in midstride. ''Not on my account.''

Alex added, ''Don't bother.'' He stared hard at his friend. ''Grant came by to—'' He laughed. ''Why did you come by?''

Gillian read discomfort in his friend's stance as if he'd rather not say, then he rushed words. ''I came by to remind you about tonight.''

Alex looked stymied. ''Tonight? What about it?''

Grant's eyes darted to her, then back to Alex before he answered in a half whisper, ''We, uh, had a previous arrangement, Alex. Remember?'' Again his eyes darted to Gillian, then went back to him. ''Allison Granger.''

''Allison who—oh, damn.'' Alex shot a look at her, too. ''My date for tonight,'' he informed her.

Date? A feeling that teetered too close to jealousy to suit her straightened her spine.

"He's not thrilled," Grant said. "Can you tell?"

Nearby, sitting on the arm of the sofa, Alex sort of grimaced. "A blind date."

"It should be a good one," Grant was quick to say. "You have a lot in common with her. I told you that she's a paleontologist. She just came back from the Sonora Desert, something about finding fossilized bone fragments from a—" He looked stumped about the name of the dinosaur.

"Sonorasaurus thompsoni," Alex finished for him.

Gillian delivered her best smile. For a paleontologist that might be exciting, she guessed, certain now she'd misinterpreted her own feelings a second ago.

"Yes, that's right." Grant rolled his eyes. "He remembers everything," he said confidentially to Gillian even though Alex was right beside them.

"Yes, I know," she said, going along with the kidding. Along with a Mensa-caliber intellect, Alex possessed a photographic memory.

"I understand that she may join the group that's going to Turkey next week. This man," Grant said, gesturing at Alex, "turned down the opportunity to head the expedition, even though a team of archaeologists are hoping to find a cache of 1,900 silver pieces from the fifth century B.C."

"Oh, Alex." Her happiness for him was fleeting. Confused, she whirled around to face him. "You were asked and...?"

"He was asked and refused," Grant said more emphatically.

She wanted to ask why. She remembered that he'd loved field work. To lead an expedition had been a dream of his.

"Gillian's here for a reason," Alex said, taking control of the conversation and directing it away from himself.

Funny, she hadn't thought at all about why she'd come. All morning she'd been thinking only about Shelby or him.

"How long she stays might depend on you," Alex said to his friend. "We're trying to get information about someone we think taught at the university a couple of decades ago. You know more people there than I do. Who should I talk to?"

"Oh, Jane Endoff, the librarian. I think she's been there since the university first opened. Kidding, of course," Grant said, laughing at his own joke. "She's not that old. However, she might be able to help you. Are you a teacher?"

"She's been everything else," Alex answered for her. "A model, a waitress, a fund-raiser, a maid, a bookkeeper, an air courier, a small-plane pilot." He cast an askance glance her way. "Am I forgetting anything?"

She wondered how stuffy Alex's friend might be. "I delivered singing birthday messages," she said about an occupation she knew others viewed as odd and unusual.

The man's smile widened. "You really did that?" he asked with genuine interest.

"Really did that."

"And now she's off to Hawaii after leaving here," Alex informed him.

"I have a job with an air taxi service. Flying small planes from island to island sounded like fun." For a while she'd do that until something else came along.

"Always on the go." Alex added.

She accepted his kidding good-naturedly. He, more than anyone, understood her desire to live life to the fullest. As a young child she'd had a heart murmur, and her activities had been curtailed. Though eventually her heart had strengthened and her life had become normal, she'd told him once that she'd vowed during those times before her tenth birthday to make up for all the fun she'd missed.

"What time did you tell Allison I'd meet her?" Alex questioned his friend.

"At seven. And I need to leave. Deanna, my wife," Grant said for Gillian's benefit, "is making beef Stroganoff tonight. A favorite of mine. You will be on time for the date, won't you, Alex?"

"You have a tendency to nag, Grant."

"Deanna says the same thing," he said rather proudly.

Alex walked him to the door. He was shutting it when Shelby came out of her bedroom. "Daddy, can I go down to Mrs. Yabanski's? She said she was going to make chocolate-chip cookies today. She

said I could have some. Come down anytime, she
said.''

Laughing, Gillian touched the top of her head.
''I'll walk downstairs with her,'' she volunteered.
Aware now he had other plans for dinner, she con-
sidered what Shelby wanted to do. ''To make sure
Loretta's home.''

Shelby tipped her head up. ''She's home, Gillian.''

Shelby was right, Gillian knew the moment she
opened the door and the aroma of melted chocolate
wafted on the air. She waited while Shelby bounded
down the steps to the door at the first-floor landing.
Assured she was with Loretta, she reentered the
apartment. She found Alex standing at the open refrigerator door. ''Shouldn't you be getting ready for
your date?'' She wanted him to be happy, she reminded herself. That meant finding someone to love.

''I have to make Shelby dinner first.''

''I'll do it.''

''Thanks.'' He suddenly stood near, his eyes on
hers. He had that look again as if he was going to
kiss her.

Do it, she wanted to say. Do it, so I stop thinking
about it. ''Was Loretta supposed to baby-sit?''

''I asked her.''

Gillian scrambled to think about anything but his
nearness as his warm breath fluttered across her face.
''I'll call her, and tell her that I'll sit with Shelby,
but Loretta can have dinner with us, if she wants.''

''Don't you want to go out?'' The small frown on

his face deepened. "You've never been the stay-at-home type."

"That was a lot of years ago." *And the one person I want to be with has a date.* "Before Scott." Scott Olney. A name from the past. Months ago, by mutual consent, they'd ended their relationship. She hadn't thought about him since that day when they'd called it quits. He'd wanted more than she'd been willing to give, he'd told her. He hadn't wanted to wake up one morning and have her announce she was leaving. His words had surprised her. She'd really thought he hadn't wanted more than good times together. He liked to be on the move, the way she did. They'd shared the excitement of sky-diving, canoeing and bungee-jumping. Thrills were fine, he'd said, but he wouldn't find something else with her that he'd wanted—a long-term relationship. "Are you worried I'll be an old maid?" she asked Alex.

"You're good with Shelby. You should have kids of your own."

She didn't want to analyze herself. "Blame it on the first guy I thought I loved," she said in a light tone.

He inclined his head as if to see her face better. "Thought?"

How could she explain? There had never really been anyone. "The first guy was a jerk."

"Why was he a jerk?"

She'd been so young, so easily impressed back then. "He played basketball for the high school team. I thought he was wonderful. So did he," she said airily now, recalling the memory with amusement. "He was so full of himself."

"Then who came along?"

"No athlete." She opened a cupboard, scanned cans. "I swore off them. And chose this rather nerdy-looking guy in the science club."

"Someone like me?"

She gave up her visual search of the cupboard's contents and faced him. "You're not nerdy."

"You used to think so."

She squinched her nose at him. "Never." Males were so predictable, she mused as she noted how pleased he looked by her response.

"You really were in the science club?"

"Quit sounding so amazed. All he talked about were rocks. He was into geology. Actually he was an absolute bore, but I was trying to up my standards."

"Which one broke your heart?"

She smirked. "Neither of them."

"The love of the moment came later?" he asked, referring to Scott.

"I didn't love him, Alex. I know that now. There's never been a man I liked being with that much." *Except—except you. Him?* "You need to get ready," she said, and pointed at the clock to think about something else. "Or you'll be late." She gave him a backhand wave, tried to act casual. "You know how you hate being late," she added, urging him to leave before she did something foolish.

What Alex hated more was going on a blind date. In his bedroom he dressed slowly. He'd like to stay home tonight, make popcorn, watch a movie with Gillian. He'd like to just sit and talk with her. Possibly all the weird reactions to her had to do with her leaving soon. An ocean would separate them. She'd be gone for a long time, he reasoned.

He shoved his wallet into his back pocket and headed out of the room. "What culinary masterpiece am I missing tonight?" he asked when he reached the kitchen doorway.

Her back to him, she stood before the stove, mixing barbecue sauce into crumbled ground beef. "Sloppy joes."

"You have a mean streak, Quinn, or you wouldn't have made something tonight that I like."

She sent him a poor-you look. "Too bad. You have to go." She turned off the burner. "I called Loretta. She and Shelby like them. So that's why we're having this."

"Have fun," he muttered, heading for the door before he changed his mind. He swore he heard her soft laugh. On the way out he stopped at Loretta's, kissed Shelby goodbye and felt totally unnecessary.

"Bye, Daddy." She smacked his cheek with a wet kiss. Unlike other times, she didn't fuss about him going out.

He wished again that he could stay home.

Allison Granger was a tall brunette with a toothy smile. That was all right with Alex. He'd rather be with a smiler than a grouch. She also talked constantly. He figured she was nervous. No one liked blind dates. Why anyone agreed to them was beyond him. He supposed it came from some need to please. If a friend went to the bother to find someone they thought was perfect for you, how could you say no? The problem was that blind dates rarely worked. This was Alex's fifth. He had plenty of people at the university who were bound and determined to end his single-father days. He appreciated their concern, but he hoped no one else did him this kind of favor again.

"I really thought the movie was enjoyable," Allison said.

Gillian would have hated it, he knew.

Beside him, Allison shifted on the passenger's side of the car. In the dark confines of it he felt her eyes on him. "Did you like it?"

"Not really," he admitted. "No one said what they felt." Yeah, Gillian would hate that. She believed people should be honest.

"But that made it more thought provoking."

He shrugged, not wanting to encourage a discussion. During dinner he'd made that mistake, and Allison had offered her views through dinner and dessert about the inaccuracies of every dinosaur movie.

"They mixed Jurassic period dinosaurs with Cretaceous ones," she'd said, making it sound like the crime of the century.

He believed some movies were meant to be seen purely for their enjoyment value. He'd seen the more

famous old ones with Gillian, enjoyed her reactions
as she gripped his hand during the scariest moments,
hid her eyes behind a spread-fingered hand. He realized that was the last time he'd really enjoyed a
movie.

In a way he was grateful that Allison talked in-
cessantly. She kept conversation flowing, so they
avoided long, uncomfortable silences. He saw her to
the door, thanked her and made a quick escape before
she assumed he wanted a kiss. He wouldn't see her
again. That wasn't her fault. It was his. Maybe he
wasn't ready to date. It didn't matter that he'd been
alone for years, that he'd stopped loving Nicki before
they'd talked about a divorce. Possibly he was one
of those guys who'd had a shot at love and marriage,
the whole bit, and having blown it, wasn't supposed
to try again.

Disgusted with himself, he wasn't sure if he hoped
Gillian was still awake or not. He stepped from his
vehicle, noticed all the lights off except the living
room one. She might have left it on so he wouldn't
walk into a dark apartment. The thought that she
wasn't still awake dampened his spirits. He felt ready
to kick something by the time he unlocked the door
and stepped into the living room.

"How was the date?"

Unprepared, he gave a start. "Jeez, woman," he
muttered while he closed the door behind him.

On the sofa, her legs tucked beneath her, she shot
an impish grin at him. "Scare you?"

"Of course not. But I wasn't expecting you to still be up."

"I was knitting." She gestured at a ball of bright-blue yarn and knitting needles on the cushion beside her. "Did you have a good time tonight?"

He shrugged off his jacket. "I really hate the dating game."

"I know you do." Empathy laced her voice. "So do I. Some of the men are such clowns."

Alex pulled a face. "Allison Granger is probably saying those exact words right now."

A hint of a smile tugged at the corners of her lips. She had such a great smile, he thought not for the first time. White, even teeth. Soft lips. Were they as soft as they looked? He'd kissed her cheek. He'd hugged her, held her close. But he'd never kissed her, really kissed her.

"You didn't like her?"

How could he answer that honestly and not sound like a jerk? "She was a nice woman."

She inclined her head in a manner that was so familiar he couldn't help smiling. "Did she bore you?"

He stepped near, wanting to smell lilacs. "I probably bored her."

"On behalf of all the women who've ever dealt with insensitive males, thank you. That was a sweet thing to do."

He wasn't sure what he'd done. "What was?"

Standing, she picked up the ball of yarn. "Pretending anything that went wrong was your fault."

"It was." Though tempted, he sidestepped an urge to bury his fingers in her hair. "I wanted to be somewhere else." As green eyes locked on his, he couldn't look away. "I was thinking about you." The words just came out.

"What did you say?"

Why was she lifting her mouth to his? He gave her a moment, time to draw away, place a palm against his chest to keep him at a distance. Maybe laugh. But instead of stepping back, she leaned closer. He drew in a deep breath, let her scent float over him. "I'd rather have been with you."

Chapter Five

Oh, Lord. Gillian imagined there were dozens of reasons why she should move. Instead she stood firm. She wasn't sure if he'd meant that, but he'd thrilled her. "Me?"

Since the first time she'd seen him, she'd been curious about his kiss. She'd wondered about his taste, about the heat he would stir. That fascination had lasted only until he'd angered her. Then for months they'd been at odds. She'd thought of him as the fuddy-duddy bookworm. He'd viewed her as the zany redhead. She'd had no desire to talk to him, much less kiss him. When she'd finally stopped disliking him at that Utah dig, the idea of kissing him promised to spoil what they'd found.

And now she had plans, didn't need complications.

He was her friend, her buddy, someone she'd been able to depend on, someone she needed a different way. "I wondered about us, too," she heard herself admitting. "I mean it's natural that we'd—"

"Be curious." His palm on the small of her back held her in place.

Against her breast she felt the thudding hardness of his heart. "Yes." He expelled a long breath, the heat of it fanning her face. She could barely think straight. None of this made sense. Why now? She didn't want to have to leave. She didn't know what she might learn in the next few days, but she wanted Alex with her, someone who'd care about what she was feeling, who'd hold her if she needed a hug.

He started to reach forward as if he was going to touch her face, but stopped himself. A hint of humor edged his voice. "This would be a mistake, wouldn't it?"

Would it? How could he be so sure of that? Did he believe that or was he working hard to convince himself?

He pressed his forehead to hers. "Gillian, I don't want to lose you as a friend."

No, she didn't want that, either. But an attraction existed, maybe had smoldered beneath the surface since they'd first met. Would one kiss hurt? Don't think about that. Because she didn't know how else to handle the moment, with feigned formality, she straightened her shoulders and held out her hand for a handshake to seal the deal. "Friends?"

As she'd hoped, he released a quick, short laugh.

Tightly he caught her hand in his, then brought it to his lips and kissed her palm. "Always."

Despite that lighthearted moment, she wondered how he would act this morning. After slipping on a loose, gray sweatshirt, black jogging pants and sneakers, she dashed outside. Cool morning air and a cloudy sky promised rain. Uneasy about seeing Alex, she looked for an outlet to rid herself of nervous energy and ran for an extra mile.

Near the end of her run, she made a decision. Best friends couldn't be replaced, and she needed a friend more than a love in her life. With that thought firmly in mind, she jogged up the steps to the apartment and opened the door.

Then she saw him.

Braced against the kitchen counter, he studied her for a long moment. He looked the epitome of respectability. Dressed in gray slacks and a pale-blue button-down shirt, he'd draped a navy blazer over a chair. Since he usually dressed casually for class, she assumed he had a meeting with college bigwigs.

Another silent moment passed. What should she say? Though his eyes appeared like slits, she could feel their intensity.

"Are we really all right?" he asked suddenly.

No, she didn't think so. Otherwise, her pulse wouldn't have jumped like a warning the moment she'd seen him. "Yes, we're all right," she answered. Her reaction to him was her problem, not his.

"All right enough to meet me for dinner?"

She fought a fluttery sensation in her stomach. "I'd love to."

"Shelby's playing at Jenna's, a friend, this afternoon after preschool. I'll talk to Jenna's mother, see if she'll drop Shelby off at the restaurant." Seeming in a hurry, while he gave her a time to meet him at the faculty lounge, he headed toward the door. "See you later."

"Yes, later." She watched him leave and released the breath she'd been unaware she was holding. She believed his suggestion for dinner was his way of saying nothing had changed between them.

Voices outside Loretta's door drifted to her. Gillian guessed that Alex had stopped there to say goodbye to Shelby, who'd wait at Loretta's for Jenna's mommy to drive her to preschool. They'd all be all right, she assured herself.

For another moment she stared out the kitchen window at the huge pines and the overcast sky, then reached for the telephone.

"You're late," Grant said instead of a greeting and fell in step with Alex outside the university library. "Tell me how the date was?" he asked, not even attempting to veil his inquisitiveness.

"She's pleasant." Alex eyed his watch while he lengthened his stride to reach his classroom. He detested being late. But more bothered him this morning. He'd had to leave quickly. He'd been struggling to keep his hands off Gillian. He'd wanted to touch her hair, her cheek, skim fingers down her arm. He wanted everything that he'd convinced himself he shouldn't want.

"Does your lack of enthusiasm for Allison have anything to do with your houseguest?" A twinkle gleamed in Grant's eyes. "And don't give me that she's-a-friend business. The woman is gorgeous. And she seems intelligent."

"Extremely."

"And she must be fun to be with, or she wouldn't be a friend."

Alex slowed his stride. Where was this conversation going?

"Easy to talk to?" Grant went on.

He could tell Gillian anything, almost anything. "Yes."

Grant grabbed his arm, halting him. "Then what is the problem? No chemistry? Why aren't you interested in her?" The question came as they reached the lecture hall. "Or are you?" Grant asked on a parting note.

Alex would swear he heard his friend laugh. It was insane to let Grant's words distract him. But ten minutes into his lecture about third-millennium B.C. Egypt, he decided his day was not going to go well. One student's head bobbed. Aware of his sleeper's interest in anything sexual, he deliberately offered words to rouse him, "Cones filled with perfumed fat were worn on the heads of beautiful women to kill their body odor, and often were believed to be an aphrodisiac."

One girl's top lip curled at the idea. His sleeper peeked through slitted eyes at him. And for the first time since he'd begun teaching, he wanted to be somewhere else.

As students filed out of his room, he stacked papers and shoved them into a briefcase and let his mind wander back to Grant's words. His friend had been talking about a serious, long-term relationship for Gillian and him. He knew she'd never want that. She'd denounced wanting everything he needed in his life. But even knowing that didn't stop him from considering what-ifs. What if they let feelings deepen? What if they could be together for a while?

Alone, Gillian had called her brother. The conversation with Sean about Lenore's child was brief. Before they'd learned that Lenore's baby had died, Sean had reminded his sisters of the legalities involved if they found their father's illegitimate child. Since Rachel's phone call that the baby had died, they no longer needed to consider that.

"When are you leaving there?" he asked.

Gillian shifted the phone to her other ear and frowned, sure he wouldn't like her answer. "I'm still going to look for Lenore Selton."

"Why? There's no sibling of ours out there."

"Maybe there never was." There she'd said it. He'd run to Rachel with that news, but there was no point in lying to them about what she felt.

"What did you say?" He sounded astonished.

"Maybe there never was," she repeated. "I need to be face-to-face with Lenore, question her, find out if she was telling the truth about being pregnant with Dad's child."

"Sometimes people are unfaithful."

She was silent for a second. He'd suffered enough pain at the hands of someone who'd claimed to love him. "I don't believe Dad was." She heard irritation in her voice and drew a calming breath.

"No matter how close we are to someone, we don't really know another person," he reminded her.

She had no doubt now that he was thinking about his ex-wife, about Cassie's lies, about his life.

"What does all of this mean? You'll dig around to get answers?"

"Exactly."

"And what if you find out that Dad was unfaithful?"

"I'll have to accept that, won't I?"

"Gillian, it might be easier on you to accept that now." Pragmatic, always, he faced life head-on. Criminal law had swept away youthful idealism.

"I can't," she answered. She led with her heart, could easily be hurt. But she had to follow through on her feelings about their father. "I'd rather carry hope and be disappointed than not give him the benefit of the doubt."

A smile swept into his voice. "Why do I try? You do what you want. Do your search and keep me informed. I love you, sis."

"The feeling is mutual."

Determined to keep her mind on why she'd really come to visit and to get answers, after their goodbye she showered, then changed into a long, flowered, blue skirt and a snug cream-colored top with a boat neck and long sleeves. She'd already scanned the city's telephone directory that was in Alex's apartment and had come up empty.

At the local library, as she'd hoped, old telephone directories were available, but the phone books in storage dated back only five years, not twenty-six, and she found no Selton in any of them.

A touch discouraged, she left for the university to meet Alex. Hoping Alex had talked to the school librarian, she zipped her car into the university parking lot.

She was feet from the faculty lounge building when she saw him outside the building. She started to wave, then dropped her arm to her side. With him was a pretty brunette. In heels she stood at eye level with his six feet. He smiled at something she said but appeared uneasy.

To give him time alone with her, Gillian veered left. She would tour the school, then come back.

"Gillian," he called out before she'd taken a few steps away. Wearing a tight smile, he directed the woman's attention toward her.

He didn't need privacy; he needed rescuing, Gillian realized. A shift in his stance, a tilt of his head a certain way, a strained smile spoke volumes to her.

He waited until she was only feet from them, then made an introduction. "This is Allison Granger."

Ah, the blind date. Gillian smiled, offered a hand.

The woman received both, but her eyes had turned icy. She's interested; he's not. And she views me as a threat, Gillian mused. A day ago, she'd have laughed at the idea.

"Allison, I'll tell Grant you asked about getting symphony tickets."

"Fine. Thank you."

Almost proprietarily, he slipped a hand beneath Gillian's elbow, and anticipation slithered through her. "Ready to go?"

"I am." She offered Allison a "nice to meet you" comment, then moved with Alex toward the parking lot.

"Let's take your car. We can pick mine up on the way home later."

Unsettled, Gillian nodded. "You drive," she said, and handed him the keys to the rental car. Hands brushed. She braced herself for more sensation and averted her eyes, fearful he'd see a difference in the way she looked at him. She wanted to think about that woman. Of course, Allison Granger was all wrong for him, she decided. He needed someone with more zest, who'd take a few chances, urge him to. He needed a woman who'd make him laugh. The stiff-looking Allison Granger would eventually evolve into a sour-looking, scowling woman. She took life too seriously to be right for him.

"Allison wants me to ask Grant if he can still get her tickets to the concert next week," he said suddenly, indicating he'd been thinking about her request. "Grant has pull, since he's with the music department."

What Allison wanted was to go with Alex.

"Why so quiet?" he asked after they'd driven several blocks.

Think fast. She could hardly tell him that she was

thinking about his love life. "Is Shelby still at Jenna's?"

"Yes." He kept his eyes on traffic while he transferred lanes. "Her mother is going to drop her off at the restaurant. I'd hoped to go to some nicer place, but Shelby reminded me that I'd promised dinner here."

Gillian smiled and regarded the red-and-white exterior of the pizza parlor, a family restaurant known for a three-cheese pizza to die for and an inside playground area kids loved. "This is fine," she said, thinking it best they skip a candlelight meal.

Before leaving the car, he shed the blazer and tie, opened the button of his shirt collar and rolled sleeves to his forearms. "Did you make your phone call?" he asked when they neared the restaurant entrance.

Twice he'd met Sean. A bit of a cynic after his divorce, unlike Alex, Sean hadn't had the gentling influence of a child to keep him from getting bitter. "My brother is against a search for Lenore." Gillian followed a family of four inside. "He's never been in favor of looking for Dad's other child."

"What did he say?" he asked, curling his fingers beneath her elbow while they searched for a table.

Had he always touched her so much? If so, why was she suddenly so aware? Gillian waited until they settled at a booth near the wall of windows, then relayed her conversation with her brother.

"Sounds as if he simply doesn't want you to get hurt."

She looked up as the waitress came to take their

order. Enough about her family, she mused. Nothing would be resolved for a while, but in the meantime, maybe she could help him with Joe. "Did you talk to your father today?"

He shifted on the booth seat to have a view of the entrance. "He probably called Loretta."

"Won't he call you?"

His eyes remained on the door to watch for Shelby. With his head angled away, his words came out muffled. "There's not much to say."

Gillian didn't believe he was so blasé about the situation. "Why can't you two talk?" she asked, trying to understand.

His shoulders rose; his back straightened fractionally. "Because we never learned to," he said simply, and for a moment she thought he would close the door on discussing his father. "Nothing was easy between us even when I was a kid," he went on. "It hasn't gotten any better. He feels forced to be here."

She felt sympathy for his father. "Alex, this must be difficult for him." His gaze came back to her. Annoyance darkened it. She didn't doubt he thought she was being disloyal for empathizing with Joe. "He's an independent man, used to moving around, Alex."

"He'll have to adjust," he said in an uncharacteristically cool tone.

More than a vagabond lifestyle, a need for roots and security must have caused such anger in him. He was a fair man, one who willingly tried to see others' viewpoints.

"He didn't give a damn about what my mother or

I felt. He moved us from one military base to another. I was always losing friends, transferring from one school to another, never having a sense of belonging.''

What had his mother thought? she wondered. She realized they'd never talked about her before. She knew Alex had loved her, had been heartbroken when she'd died. "What did your mother think of the moving around?"

"She loved him. She'd have gone wherever he wanted her to go. I was thirteen. Angry for her." He stared ahead. There was no difference in his facial expression, but his hand had tightened on the beer mug on the table before him. "My mother and I had stayed at the base in San Diego because she'd needed treatments. Joe had been in Beirut. He came home for the funeral, made arrangements for it and for me.''

"For you?" Hadn't Joe taken him with him? Surely he could have requested he be stationed stateside for his son's sake.

"He decided in less than an hour after coming home that I should go to military school. We had her funeral. The next morning he drove me to the school, then left. I don't know him. He doesn't know me. We're strangers living together. And if you asked him, he'd tell you I'm not the son he wanted.''

"Alex—"

He raised a hand, cut her off. "No matter how sorry I am that I'm such a giant disappointment to him, it won't change anything. We're strangers.''

Was he wrong? Was he misreading how his father

felt? ''I can't help wondering why you think you disappointed Joe.''

''That's obvious, isn't it? We aren't a matched set, are we? He wanted a son like himself. Mr. Macho.''

She'd always thought the man sitting near her was pretty macho, but then she'd seen him away from the university and the books. She'd seen him at a dig site, unshaven, muscular arms gleaming. She'd witnessed him rescuing another student who'd slipped off the cliff. While people had scrambled to where she was hanging on to the cliff's edge, he was the one who'd reached her first, who'd strained, using every ounce of strength and determination he possessed to hang on to her. Gritting his teeth, sweat pouring from him, he'd lifted her to safety by the time everyone had reached them. He'd been a hero.

''But you are,'' she finally said.

He released a short, mirthless laugh. ''Thanks. But that's not true.''

He didn't see himself accurately, she realized. ''Why did you refuse the opportunity to lead the fieldwork in Turkey?'' she asked, recalling Grant's words during his visit. ''It would be a thrill, something you've always wanted to do.''

''Once. Not anymore. That dream belonged to a different man. Some things are more important.'' His eyes strayed to Shelby at the door now. ''This is where I belong.''

With his daughter. Gillian suddenly wondered why she'd even asked him that question.

Shelby dashed to them, and in a rush she threw slim arms around her father's neck. ''Can I go play until we eat?'' she asked, indicating the play area for children.

"Say hi."

She pulled back, though one slim arm remained draped over his shoulder. "Hi, Gillian."

Gillian winked at her. "Can she, Daddy?"

"Go until dinner comes," he said, smiling. Before he'd finished, she'd taken off toward the other kids. Laughing, she trailed them into a colorful tunnel. He stood to talk with Jenna's mother and thanked her for bringing Shelby to them.

Gillian considered all he'd said, could think of no comforting words. She didn't know what Joe felt. Regardless, she felt so sad for both of them. Unlike Alex, she'd had a wonderful relationship with her father.

Like Shelby had with her daddy, she mused, watching Shelby at the top of the tunnel, staring through the plastic window and waving at him. "You're so lucky to have her," she said when he settled across from her again.

"I think so, too. Since the day she was born, she's been the most important thing in my life," he said softly. "I never wanted her to feel unloved or unwanted."

Gillian yearned for the right words. What could she say? As a child he'd felt that way, she knew now.

"I'm sorry about all of this. This wasn't the way I planned this evening to go. We're supposed to be talking about you. I wanted to meet you for dinner because I got information for you."

Her mind on him, she was slow to respond. "About Lenore?"

"I talked to the librarian. She didn't know Lenore, but a woman named Mildred Nevins was secretary at the university back then. And supposedly knew everyone. She also was friends with Edith Selton."

Gillian grappled to curb anxiousness, but at this moment she was closer to answers than her family had been since the day her sister first opened their mother's diary and read words that had changed the way they viewed their father. "Did you talk to her?"

"No, she's retired, but I have an address and phone number. I talked to her landlady. Mildred wasn't home. She had knee surgery recently and is recovering at her daughter's in Payson. So we don't know more."

"But we do," she said, feeling more optimistic. "Mildred will help me find Edith, then I'll learn where to find Lenore."

"I think that's one of the things I like most about you." He caught her hand that rested on the table. "You always look for the bright side of things." Unexpectedly, he leaned close and kissed her. It lasted no more than a millisecond, but long enough to deliver a hard hit to her mid-section.

"Daddy!"

With effort, Gillian focused on Shelby darting toward them. "She looks excited," she said to Alex.

He gave her a funny smile. Was he, too, still thinking about what he'd done?

Her eyes bright and shining, his daughter braked beside Alex. "Jenna's going to San Diego. She's going to see the whale and porpoises at Sea World. I wish we could go.'' She slid onto the brown vinyl bench beside Gillian and stared across the table at her father.

''Someday.''

Gillian wondered how he could refuse her anything when she turned those blue eyes on him.

Shelby heaved an enormous sigh. ''He always says that for something that's a long time away.''

''She has you figured out,'' Gillian teased.

''Too well,'' he admitted, and stretched forward across the table to swipe a finger down his daughter's nose.

Through dinner Shelby seemed quieter, Gillian thought. She said nothing to Alex, but concerned for the little one, after getting ready for bed that night, she wandered to Shelby's room to check on her. ''Shelby,'' she whispered, stepping closer. ''Are you still awake?'' she asked, though she could see she was.

''Uh-huh.''

Her concern intensifying, Gillian settled on the edge of the mattress beside her. She hoped Shelby would share with her whatever was bothering her. She doubted this had anything to do with her request to go to San Diego. ''Did your daddy read you a bedtime story?''

In the darkened room, the little girl's eyes met hers. ''Uh-huh.''

''Can you tell me what's wrong? Why you're not sleeping?''

''I got to go to school next week.''

And she's scared, Gillian guessed. "Yes, I know." Gillian brushed back her bangs. "Won't that be fun?"

"What if it isn't?"

"Oh, honey." This was getting complicated. She felt her heart opening even more, welcoming Shelby in, and ran a caressing hand over her forehead. Alex had mentioned she was starting school soon. "It's going to be fun and exciting. It always is when you do something new. And you're going to meet new people. That's what's best of all."

"It is?"

"It is," Gillian said and bent forward to kiss her cheek.

"I'm glad you're here, Gillian."

Her heart twisted. "Me, too." A need, one she hadn't ever felt before, hadn't been aware existed, raced through her. She wasn't sure what to do with it. Cuddling Shelby close, she felt as if she would burst with emotion. She simply held her, absorbed the pleasure of having a child in her arms. "Good night, sweetie."

Shelby drew back, but instead of lying down, she stared past her at the doorway. "Night, Daddy."

"How long have you been there, Daddy?" Gillian asked.

"Long enough." Alex moved forward. Since leaving the restaurant, he'd kept his distance from her, but in a thank-you gesture, he pressed a hand on Gillian's shoulder now. Thank God, she'd been here. She had a knack for saying the right thing. He would never have said that to his daughter, never given her words to offer peace of mind and alleviate her fears. He would probably have messed up, intensified her anxiety.

Smiling at both of them, he leaned over his daughter and kissed her good-night. Assured Shelby was in good hands, he pivoted away. If he were going to choose someone to bring into Shelby's life, he would wish for someone like Gillian.

But it would never be her, he knew. Like Nicki she'd be bored with the life he was living. Everything he strived for, she shunned. He needed security for himself and Shelby. He led an organized life, a predictable one, probably a dull one by Gillian's standards. His life was full of other people and responsibilities. He wouldn't have it any other way. But she didn't want to be trapped by others needing her. She was like a butterfly drifting on the wind.

Chapter Six

Clothes tumbled in the washing machine. Gillian had awakened early, and rather than stay in bed and think too much, she'd wandered through the dark apartment to the kitchen, started the coffee brewer, and after a quick run had settled with a paperback in the laundry room adjacent to the kitchen and waited for the dryer cycle to finish.

Emotions hovered close to the surface lately. About her family problem. About Shelby. About Alex. All that awareness about Alex was probably her own fault. For years she'd believed she didn't want a commitment or to get married, at least not for a while. Maybe she was lonely. That might explain the unexpected feelings for him.

Lost in thought, she looked up from her paperback

and saw Shelby quietly sitting nearby on the floor. How long had she been there? How often did she sit near Alex when he was working? ''You're very quiet,'' she said, closing the book.

''Daddy says sometimes I can be noisy, and sometimes I need to be quiet.''

''We all need to do that sometimes.'' Gillian dumped clothes from the dryer into the laundry basket. ''Want to come with me while I fold?''

She scrambled to her feet. As if receiving an okay to talk, she chattered nonstop on the way to the bedroom. ''You have pretty clothes.''

Gillian looked up from folding a sleeping shirt to see Shelby at the closet eyeing her black silk slip dress.

''This is pretty. Can I touch?''

''Sure you can.''

Her little fingers stroked the material. ''It feels nice.''

On a whim, Gillian had bought the dress in San Francisco because she'd wanted to own one dress by the famous designer.

An eager grin sprang to Shelby's face. ''You have lots of shoes.''

Actually she had a fetish for them. When her spirits drooped she purchased a new pair of shoes and felt better. ''I like shoes.''

''Daddy says he doesn't know why he buys me any.'' She giggled. ''Cause I'm always barefoot.''

Gillian looked down. Sure enough she was barefoot. ''Who painted your toenails?''

"Mrs. Yabanski. Daddy said it was okay cause it's clear. I like your color."

Gillian slid out of her slipper sandals and wiggled her toes.

"What's that color called?"

"Nice 'n' Toasty."

Her dark head bent, she tugged on the drooping waistband of the pink pajamas. "That's funny." Still looking down, she lined up her foot with one of the high-heeled sandals.

Gillian finished folding a sweatshirt. "You can try them on."

Her head shot up, her eyes went wide. "Really?"

"Really. And you can look at the costume jewelry in that bag again." She pointed to the black-and-white cosmetic bag, a freebie with some makeup she'd purchased. "You can try it on, if you want."

Shelby's eyes danced with delight at the fake strand of pearls in her hand. "Jenna's mommy lets her play dress-up with her things." She slipped the necklace over her head, then wobbled on the heels to the full-length mirror mounted behind the door and smiled at her reflection.

Gillian grabbed a straw hat with a bright yellow ribbon from the closet shelf. "That's nice of her mommy," she said, and plopped the hat on Shelby's head.

"She is nice." A thoughtful look settled over Shelby's heart-shaped face as she viewed her reflection. "My mommy didn't want me. That's why she left without me."

Gillian thought she might have misunderstood, but

the unmistakable sadness in Shelby's eyes verified that she hadn't. She honestly didn't know what to say. But she'd bet her life on one thing—Alex was too sensitive to others' feelings to have put such a notion in her head. "Shelby, who told you that?"

"I know."

Gillian heard a hostile edge in her sweet voice. "Well, I like being with you," she said to offer an assurance. "And I know your daddy does."

She nodded. "That's what he said, too."

"And Mrs. Yabanski," Gillian went on to put her in a more positive frame of mind. But it had become obvious why she wouldn't want a mommy. Another mommy might do the same thing—leave her. "And your grandpa."

"And all my stuffed animals."

"That's right. And who else?" she asked, making a game of it as Shelby faced her, smiling. "Jenna. And—"

"What's this?" Hair mussed, jaw unshaven, Alex padded in wearing only jeans, and swept an arm in Shelby's direction. "Who's your friend, Gillian?"

"Daddy, it's me!"

He faked his best surprised look. "No, it isn't."

She tittered. "Yes, it is. You're silly." She slipped off the heels and dashed to him. "Gillian let me try on her beads," she said, touching the long strand hanging at her neck as he scooped her up. "She's nice."

"I think so, too." He spoke softly to her as if they were alone, and he was telling her a secret. "And she promised to make breakfast today."

It took a moment for Gillian to focus on conversation, to drag her gaze away from the firm lines of his broad chest, from smooth, masculine flesh. "I did?" she said, sending him a narrow-eyed gaze.

At her feigned indignant tone, he barely held back a smile. "Thank you for offering."

"You're welcome." She sent him a "you'll pay" look. "Is that how you persuade students to do something? You volunteer them?"

He cracked a smile. "Sometimes it works."

As he disappeared, Shelby tugged on her hand. "Daddy likes pancakes best."

"That's nice." Gillian let herself be led toward the kitchen. She was not the best pancake maker. "I'll make French toast. Okay?"

"I like French toast." Shelby beamed up at her. "Lots. Can I help?" she asked as Gillian removed a frying pan from a cabinet.

She couldn't resist reaching out, touching the top of Shelby's dark hair. "Sure you can. Do you know what else we can do?" Angling away, she switched on a radio located in a corner of the counter and turned the dial until she tuned in to a station playing an old rock and roll tune. "I'll teach you to twist."

Shelby's eyes widened. "Twist?"

Gillian demonstrated a few of the steps to the popular old dance. "Like this."

As she'd expected, Shelby giggled behind a hand.

By the time the bacon was sizzling and a stack of French toast was in the warming oven, Shelby had mastered the dance steps.

Her laughter mingling with Gillian's, she stopped

suddenly when she saw her father in the kitchen doorway. "Daddy, look what I'm doing. It's fun. You do it."

Alex turned a squinty-eyed look on her. "I'm not doing *that*."

Conspiratorially Gillian bent to Shelby's level and whispered loud enough for him to hear. "Daddy doesn't dance. But he could learn."

Alex ignored her completely. "What smells so good?"

A hand on her hip, Gillian waited for him to look her way, then smirked. "Don't you want to discuss your dancing ability?"

"No," he said, appearing pleased with himself. "But I'll say thank you for a different reason."

She understood. Without a mommy influence, Shelby didn't get to do this often with another female, which Gillian guessed was his real reason for volunteering her to make breakfast and his thank you.

"I assumed you'd want to see Mildred." He nudged Shelby's chair closer for her, then sat. "So I called her, asked if it was okay if we come tomorrow."

"You did?" Sitting across from him, she offered him the platter of French toast. "Thank you, but do you have time?"

"I have time."

She'd wanted him to say that, but she knew he must have a dozen things that needed his attention.

"Daddy, I got to go," Shelby whispered. "Peepee." With his nod she scooted off her chair.

"Alex." Gillian had to say what was on her mind. "Tell me you have nothing to do."

Alex raised his gaze from the plate of food. "Except be with you for this. Don't you want me along?"

His words quickened her heart. *More than you know.* "I do. I really do, but I feel guilty, too. I don't want you to turn your life topsy-turvy for me."

She thought she had a grip on the moment, then he leaned forward, caught her chin and held her face still. "You're worried, aren't you?"

She couldn't pretend with him. "A little."

"That's a good enough reason for me to be with you."

She flushed, realized she might be making too much of his words, but they pleased her more than she'd expected.

"I'm back," a small voice sang as if they wouldn't notice.

Looking amused, Alex chuckled. "She makes such demure entrances."

Gillian smiled with him. She'd meant what she'd said. She didn't want to upset his world in any way, or jeopardize their friendship.

"I'm going to learn lots of things when I start school," Shelby announced with enthusiasm.

"Fun things," Gillian told her. "And you'll probably have a teacher as nice as your daddy."

That sparked a bigger smile on her face.

"What are your students learning about, Professor?" she asked, wanting to think about something other than her reaction to him or tomorrow and what Mildred might tell her.

He poked his fork into another piece of French toast. "Pharaohs of Egypt."

Gillian clung to the small talk. "Ah, Ramses II and Akhenaton."

"We're discussing the influence of Nefertiti."

Shelby offered her opinion. "Those are funny names."

Gillian was glad to have her there, distracting. For the next few moments she rambled on about friends' names. As she finished eating, she gave up on the list, and with an excuse-me, she dashed out of the room.

"She's done so well. Because of you." Gillian meant that but a problem did exist, and she wasn't certain he was aware of it.

"I can't take credit. She did well because she was young when Nicki died. She didn't even know her."

"Little ones forget."

"How old were you when you lost your parents?" he asked, wandering toward the laundry room. "Twelve?"

"Eleven. I was heartbroken." She sipped her coffee. "But as hard as that was for Sean and me, it was hardest for Rachel." She'd told him before how her sister, at nineteen, had accepted being guardian to a teenager and a little girl.

Rachel had never complained about her life. Still Gillian believed her sister had to have regrets. She'd taken on responsibilities when she should have been spreading her wings, enjoying life, sampling new experiences. She'd deserved a life of her own, but had been too tied down to look for that until her late twenties. And during those years what had she wanted that had eluded her? What did she regret? Gillian had no answer to those questions. But she knew she'd never have regrets. Long ago, she'd vowed that she'd do everything she wanted before settling down. "It couldn't have been easy for Rachel," she said, joining him in the other room. "She sacrificed a lot for us." Too much, Gillian believed.

Standing by a small Formica table, he held a pair of Shelby's socks. "You told me that Rachel's happy."

"Oh, yes." Her sister sounded ecstatic whenever she talked about Kane and Heather. "She has a good life now. She's happily married and has a family of her own. She loves Heather, Kane's niece, like her own, and Kane has given her all the happiness I'm sure she thought she'd never know." She watched him stack a towel on top of others she'd folded earlier. "I didn't finish."

"You didn't have to fold any of our clothes."

"I didn't mind." Too aware of his nearness, she snatched up another towel.

"Thanks for doing this." He kept looking at her with the same intensity she'd seen before. "And for breakfast."

One real kiss and she'd be cured of all this fantasizing. Could he tell she was thinking about it? She looked down at the blue terry cloth in her hands. "My pleasure." *Stop thinking so much. Talk about Shelby.* Ever since those moments with Shelby in the bedroom, she'd wondered how to bring up what his daughter had said. *Jump in feet first.* "I need to talk to you about something that happened earlier."

He set one of Shelby's tops aside. "Sounds serious. What's the problem?"

It occurred to her that he might not be aware of Shelby's feelings. "Shelby said something." Stalling, she reached for a pair of Shelby's socks, folded them.

His hand closed over one of hers, stopping her actions. "About what?"

"This is hard." She raised her head, met his stare. "Are you aware of what Shelby thinks about Nicole?"

"And that is?"

Gillian repeated Shelby's words.

Softly he swore under his breath. "I'd hoped she didn't still feel that way."

The hum of the washing machine stopped. "You knew?"

"Sort of," he admitted, opening the door on it. "Some time ago an acquaintance made a remark. Unaware Shelby was near, the woman said Nicki was a lousy mother. After all, what kind of mother doesn't want her child?"

A sick sensation settled in the pit of her stomach as she visualized Shelby listening to those words. "That was an awful thing for Shelby to hear."

Pain for his daughter shadowed his eyes. "The person hadn't meant to hurt Shelby. She was offering me sympathy, in her own way. I hadn't realized that Shelby had heard."

"When did this happen?" Gillian asked, grabbing

a bundle of wet clothes and transferring them to the dryer.

"About six months ago."

"Before that, what did she think?"

He closed the dryer door. "She thought that her mommy had gone to heaven. I didn't think a child under four needed to hear all the rest, and that Nicki had left us before she died."

"What did she say to you after hearing the woman?"

"She was too quiet during the drive home. You know what a yakker she can be." He pushed in the button on the dryer. "When I asked her what was wrong, she wanted to know if I lied to her."

"Oh, Alex."

"Yeah. That hit me hard. What parent wants their kid to believe he's a liar? I told her no that I hadn't. I wouldn't lie to her. Her mommy was in heaven. She didn't say a word. I figured she was waiting for me to explain. So I did. I told her that before her mother died she did move away. She had someplace to go where it would be hard for her to take a baby, so we decided that Shelby stay with me."

Returning to the folding table, she held up one of Shelby's T-shirts, bud-green with a turtle on it. "Did she accept that?"

"I thought so. But if she said that to you, then she must not have accepted what I said. I told her that I wanted her as much as a mommy and daddy. I thought that was the right thing to say."

Gillian folded a pillowcase. "Shelby has it in her head now that she doesn't need a mommy."

"So nothing has changed. She told me that if her

mommy didn't want her, then she didn't want one.'' A hint of the misery he was feeling threaded into his voice. "I don't know how to undo the damage. And finding the right woman isn't easy. I chose poorly once already.''

He'd never said anything like that before. "You've always been too hard on yourself.'' She couldn't help wondering. "Do you regret marrying her?''

"How can I? If I hadn't, I wouldn't have Shelby. But you know what Nicki was like.''

Gillian had never liked her, had thought Alex could have done better. But the feeling had been mutual. Not wanting to cause trouble between him and his wife, Gillian had kept her distance after he married Nicole. She remembered a phone call from him, the challenge and hurt in his voice when he questioned why he hadn't heard from Gillian. Under pressure she'd finally told him why.

"You're my friend. I'm not giving you up,'' he'd said.

But then he'd learned Nicole was pregnant. He hadn't wanted to upset her. They'd agreed to cool the friendship. Three months after the baby was born, Alex revealed Nicole wanted a divorce. She'd felt smothered being a professor's wife and wanted her freedom to enjoy life. Aware how much he loved the baby, Gillian was relieved for him when he disclosed that Nicole believed the baby would have a more stable life with him. She announced she would never be back and took off for Europe and a new boyfriend's villa. Before Shelby turned one, Nicole died in a boating accident.

"She wasn't happy."

Gillian knew he'd been stunned when he'd realized that. Nicki had seemed perfect to him. He'd met her at a faculty party and they were married soon after. Her uncle, a banker, had been a good friend of one of his colleagues. Before he and Nicole had married, she'd pretended to like the academic life. Afterward, she'd complained constantly about the sameness of her days. But no matter how much she detested living that life, how could she walk away from her baby?

"She was furious when she learned she was pregnant. I convinced her to have the baby, told her that I would take care of it and she could be free."

"You'd already talked about divorce?"

"Yes. But I knew what it was like to have a father who didn't give a damn about me. I made a promise that I'd give the baby more of a home life than I had. I believe she needs a mommy. But for Shelby's sake, the next marriage has to last."

How stupid Nicole was. Shelby was so sweet, so wonderful. Alex was such a wonderful man. "What kind of woman are you looking for?"

"Someone honest." He stared at the small pink shirt in his hand. "Superwoman. Someone who'll love my daughter as if she were her own. Someone who'll endure Joe and pretend to like him. Someone who'll listen to me even when I'm acting like a pontificating fool. Someone who'll want me as much as I want her."

And someone who wants to stay here and share his life. Gillian looked his way, her eyes falling on the sexy-looking, navy briefs in his hands. Did he wear them or pajamas to bed? Or nothing?

Mentally she shook her head at the thought. The last thing she needed to do was wonder what he wore to bed. That was his fault, she assured herself. Staid and serious college professors weren't supposed to walk around in sexy underwear.

"And she needs to be a rich, sexy woman," he said suddenly, seeming determined to lighten the moment.

She laughed at the comical leer he gave her, more than at his words. "Of course."

"A willowy redhead who laughs a lot," he went on, arching a brow.

Though she knew better, the comment made in jest thrilled her. "Be serious," she chided. He was teasing, she reminded herself. He hadn't meant that.

"I am serious." As his fingers slid beneath her hair and curled behind her neck, her heart quickened. With maddening slowness, his mouth caressed her brow, her cheek, her jaw. "Say no now," he murmured against her flesh.

Impatience rushed her. "I can't." For the past few days she'd thought often about him kissing her, and she suddenly didn't care what the consequences were. She pressed herself hard against him a second before his mouth closed over hers.

With a hunger she'd never expected from him, he dragged her close, pressed his lips to hers—warm, firm, demanding and coaxing. The kiss deepened, stirring every feminine need within her. His mouth challenged her, his hands skimmed her, seduced her. The kiss surpassed anything her imagination could have evoked. It made her legs feel liquid, her head spin. She thought he'd never surprise her. He did more. He excited. He aroused. He took her breath away.

How was it possible to feel so much so quickly? She felt as if she was drowning, struggling for breath. She slid her hand to his back, gripped his shirt, clung. Her heart thudded hard as if it would burst through her chest. She thought she'd be satisfied to know his taste. Now she wanted his touch. Not even with Scott had there been this hunger, this craving. She needed time to rest, yet murmured a protest when he broke the kiss.

Under his breath he swore.

Through a fog of sensation she heard the ringing phone. Only one thought grabbed hold. Had they jeopardized a wonderful friendship in one impulsive moment? Her pulse pounding like a drum, she stretched for a deep breath. "Don't be sorry," she managed unevenly.

Before she changed her mind and threw herself at him for another kiss, she pulled out of his reach. "I'd better check on Shelby." Quickly she turned away, moved through the kitchen on weak limbs to the doorway.

Behind her, he snatched up the phone, silencing the rings. "Gillian."

In midstride she stopped. *Don't say you're sorry. Don't tell me to forget it.* With all the effort she could muster, she made herself look back at him.

"Only a fool would be sorry he kissed you," he said softly.

Chapter Seven

Those words stayed with her. Because of classes and meetings Alex came home late that evening, allowing Gillian to avoid seeing him. She thought that would be best. They needed time and distance to make sense of everything.

But she went to bed thinking about those words, awakened remembering them. Edgy, wondering how he'd act, Gillian dressed and decided to skip the cozy breakfast scene this morning. She really believed that they'd be all right once they got past their first moment together. So what if the kiss had been wonderful. So what if the memory of his taste lingered. They'd forget about the kiss. She had to forget about it, not make too much of it. It couldn't mean anything.

* * *

"Is it time to go, Daddy? Is it?" Shelby's blue eyes pinned him. She'd bounded into his bedroom with a rush of words. "Jenna's mommy said it was okay if I came early. If it's okay with you. Is it?"

Alex yawned, wished she'd give him a moment to grab a cup of coffee this morning. Since he'd come home yesterday and received the call from Jenna's mother about the sleepover, his daughter had been hounding him.

Propping himself up on an elbow, he squinted at the digital clock on the bedside table and groaned. Seven-thirty was too early for a weekend wake-up. She usually gave him another hour. "She didn't mean this early, Shelby."

Rather than reprimand her for the too-early wake-up, he ran a hand over the back of her silky hair. He didn't want to sweep away the hopeful look on her face. Children were supposed to be happy, to be filled with anticipation.

"Mrs. Walders said it was okay. When I went before, it was early."

"It was nine o'clock, not seven-thirty. Come on and cuddle." He pulled her down beside him. She'd had her first sleepover weeks ago, and though he trusted Susan Walders, Jenna's mother, he still had trouble letting his daughter out of his sight for the night.

"When?" she beseeched, putting her face nose to nose with his.

He couldn't help but laugh. "After breakfast."

"Is it time for breakfast now?"

He gave in. "I guess so."

With that she bounced off the bed and danced in place. "She said that she'd call you this morning. That's why I woke you up early, so you'd be wide awake when she called you. I'll go tell Gillian that it's time now for breakfast."

Gillian wouldn't be thrilled. Most likely she was still sleeping. Wearing what? That skimpy orange thing, or the lacy peach number he'd noticed when she'd done her laundry. It had sent his mind racing and thrust his libido into high gear.

"Daddy?"

He was grateful his daughter wasn't a mind reader. He watched her whip around toward the door, then dropped his head to the pillow again and closed his eyes. An image of flowing red hair, fiery in the sunshine came to mind. He saw Gillian perched on the edge of a friend's boat years ago. Relaxed. Beautiful.

"Daddy!" His daughter's impatience flared again. "You said you'd get up."

As she jumped on the bed, he groaned. "I'm up. I'm up. Go."

"Do you promise?"

"I promise."

That seemed to satisfy her. Alone, Alex rolled to the edge of the bed. Eyes still partly closed, he sat up. How would it be with Gillian this morning? For someone who'd felt no spark with any woman for years, how could he ignore the explosion she'd detonated within him?

He tugged on jeans, then shrugged into a chambray shirt, was buttoning the middle buttons when the phone rang.

"It's Joe," Gillian yelled out.

He grabbed the receiver in his room. As he'd expected the call was short, less than three minutes. In a more sour mood he sat on the edge of the mattress and drew several deep breaths. Grant always said that worked for him when he was tense.

Alex gave the theory three breaths. Then swore. It was dumb to let a phone call upset him. Forget about it, he berated himself and stood. He finished buttoning his shirt, and in a better mood wandered toward the kitchen. The smell of coffee greeted him.

Standing in front of the open refrigerator door, her face partially hidden, Gillian dangled a bunch of grapes. She wore denims and an olive-green, scoop-necked T-shirt that bared her midriff. His gaze lingered at the sliver of soft flesh at her waist. Desire, quick and sharp, spread through his body. As enticing as that was, he badly needed to see her eyes, to know if her feelings for him had changed. A creak of a floorboard beneath his foot made her look over her shoulder. He tried a smile. "Good morning."

"Morning. I didn't expect you. It's early."

He wanted to step behind her, brush her hair from the nape of her neck, kiss the curve leading toward her shoulder.

"I'll be back soon," she said, shutting the refrigerator. "That's when we're leaving. Right?"

That she was halfway to the back door made him ask, "What's going on here?"

He watched her draw a deep breath. "I need to

leave early. I saw a sale for CDs in the newspaper. It's at a store nearby. I want to be first in line.''

"Do we have a problem? Are you sorry?'' he asked now, refusing to let her leave before he knew where he stood with her.

"How can I be?'' She released a quick, nervous laugh. "I wanted it.''

Her words spread warmth through his gut. The memory of a kiss was a breath away, he realized in that second. If he closed his eyes, he could summon up her taste, the feel and pressure of her lips on his. He could do something ridiculous, and say to hell with everything, grab her and kiss her again.

"I'm ready,'' Shelby announced, dragging her backpack. "Where are you going, Gillian?''

"To the store.'' She bent down, kissed Shelby's forehead. "Have fun at Jenna's.''

Alex frowned at her quick departure. She'd breezed out the door as if she was being chased. This hadn't gone as well as he'd hoped.

"I really like her, Daddy.''

Cautiously he sipped the coffee he'd just poured. "Me, too.'' Though he took delight in his daughter's company, he enjoyed being alone, had never yearned for another person until this moment. Gillian hadn't been gone five minutes and he was missing her.

Don't get used to having her around, he warned himself. She wasn't staying. She wanted to leave. She always did. Nothing he said would change that.

Barefoot, he shuffled to the counter and opened a silverware drawer. For Shelby's and Gillian's sake as well as his own, he couldn't afford to let feelings deepen.

Too excited to eat, Shelby only wanted cereal. She downed it quickly and pleaded that they leave. Alex made one phone call first to Jenna's mother. Then at eight-thirty, he drove her to Jenna's house. Fortunately Susan Walders understood the impatience level of a five-year-old and greeted them as if they were supposed to be there.

Shelby gave him a quick hug and wet kiss on the cheek, then dashed off with Jenna.

On the way home, he stopped at the grocery store, bought another box of his daughter's favorite cereal, the one that resembled miniature chocolate-chip cookies, and a new Stephen King book. Gillian loved being spooked.

He'd put away the purchases by the time she returned. In response to the door opening, he shut a cabinet door and looked over his shoulder. "Did you get what you wanted?" He motioned his head at the bag dangling from her hand, tried to ignore the urge to go to her and hold her until she relaxed against him. He hated the undercurrent of tension existing between them.

"I was successful."

Temptation skittered through him to frame her face with his hands, kiss her. "Which store did you go to?"

"The music center near the university. Even though it opened early it was packed." She plopped the bag on a chair and bent forward. Hair tumbled around her face as she dug in the white plastic bag and withdrew the CD. Snug denim strained across her backside.

Damn. Everywhere he looked, he saw something to flare desire.

"This one is no longer available in big cities." A pleased grin curved her lips. "I'd hoped I'd get it here. It's for Reed."

Though still taunting himself with thoughts of burying his face in silky strands, Alex scowled at her words about her friend in Hawaii. "What is it?"

In answer, she held up what appeared to be a CD of a Spanish guitarist.

"He likes that?"

Amusement brightened her eyes. "He says it's great mood music."

Would he use it with her? Music for seduction. Damn, he didn't like the sound of that at all.

"Are you ready to go, or do you have something else to do first?"

"We can leave." He worried about her, worried she'd learn something that might hurt her, didn't want her to be alone if that happened.

Gillian sent him another smile. She'd been so uncertain how to act this morning and hated the strain between them. They couldn't pretend to be like brother and sister anymore. One kiss had changed everything. How much had it changed? Where did they go from here? "Alex, I'm glad you're with me today. I wouldn't want what happened—"

He closed the space between them, wanted to kiss her again. "Forget about that. Right now we have

something else to think about," he said, fighting feelings.

As he drew her into his arms, she wrapped her
arms around his back and rested her cheek against
his. This—his steadiness—was what she'd been
looking for all morning. Thank you, she said silently.

Still, anxiety about the meeting shadowed her.
Every time she considered what the woman might
say, nerves fluttered in her stomach. Then again, Mildred Nevins might know nothing.

Trying to think about something else once they'd
settled in his vehicle, she opened the paperback that
Alex had set in her lap. Within minutes she was so
caught up in the tale about a woman alone in a California coastal house during a hurricane that she was
slow to look up when he slowed his Bronco. She
noted that they'd gone only a few blocks. "Is something…?"

"Look there," he said before she asked.

As he braked, her gaze swept past the For Sale
sign to the perfect-looking Victorian with its steep,
irregularly shaped roofs, a tower, the bay window
and the wraparound porch. There was even a swing
on it and a flower garden of colorful late-summer
blossoms to the side of the house. "I'm wondering
how big it is," he said absently as if speaking his
thought aloud.

She noticed an addition had been built on the back,
making the shape of the house an *L*. "Are you thinking about buying it?"

"It's not far from the university." He switched off

the ignition, his eyes riveted to the building. ''It doesn't look too small.''

Gillian noticed a birdhouse in one of the trees. ''My sister would love this house.''

He unbuckled his seat belt and reached for his cell phone on the console between them, then punched out the number that was on the sign. ''Do you mind if we wait for the real estate agent?''

Actually she was glad for a distraction. If she thought about the house, she might chase away niggling doubts about her father, might stop recalling the kiss. ''No, of course not.''

''This could be an answer to my problems.''

As she listened to him ask a few questions on the phone, she was surprised by his actions. He usually pondered longer over decisions.

''The agent will be here in a few minutes,'' he said when finished with the call. ''I know you're anxious to see Mildred, but I'd like to look at it.''

She stared out the window at the two-story building. ''It's a beautiful-looking old house.'' She meant that. The house had charm.

Within minutes a man dressed in brown plaid pants, a yellow shirt and a bolo tie arrived. Slight and balding, he peered over his wire-rimmed glasses at them. ''Your first house?'' he asked, casting a look from Gillian to Alex.

''I'm buying it alone.'' He explained his situation, told the man about his three-generation family while Gillian dealt with the funny feeling the man's initial assumption about her and Alex had stirred.

The house was bigger than it looked from the outside. Besides four bedrooms, it had a small den, a formal dining room and the living room. The home conveyed a welcoming warmth from the large windows and shining oak floors with varnished moldings to the brick fireplace and high ceilings.

Gillian followed Alex in to a bathroom. "Do you like it?" she whispered because the agent hovered near in the hallway.

"I like it," he said, turning on a bathroom spigot.

Ever helpful, Gillian flushed a toilet.

Nearby Alex squatted and eyed a pipe inside a vanity cabinet.

She bent over, saw him running fingertips along the pipe and leaned closer to speak against his ear. "What are you looking for?"

"Leaks."

As he turned his face up to hers, her eyes locked on his. A fraction closer and their mouths would touch. How insane this was. They were discussing plumbing, and she was battling desire. For one long moment he riveted her to the spot with a look, his breath heating her face. And she wanted—wanted him and everything he represented.

Stop this, she berated herself. She would tire of the town, of the sameness, within weeks. This wasn't what she wanted. It wasn't. It really wasn't. Still, she drew an unsteady breath, had to nudge herself to pull back, move away.

Not looking back, she preceded him into the kitchen, a mostly white room with a bay window that looked out on a huge yard of trees. Hopefully he hadn't noticed how strange she was acting.

Behind her, Alex offered his hand to the agent. "I'll call you. I need to think this over."

Now that was the cautious Alex she knew. "Well?" she asked the moment they were alone.

"I like it." He cupped a hand beneath her elbow during their walk on the path to his SUV. "It needs work, but it's worth the effort."

She smiled to herself. He'd fix the house, make it a home for them, just as he would mend the rift between his father and him and make them and Shelby a family. Other people made problems; he solved them.

"What do you think?"

She swept another glance at it. "I think it's a lovely old house."

"So you'd want to live there?"

Don't make too much of his question. He'd wanted her opinion that's why he asked. "I loved the French doors in the dining room that lead into the backyard." She thought it was wonderful, lush and green with several oak and pine trees. "You could string a hammock between the trees."

Humor colored his voice. "A good reason to buy the house."

How differently they looked at things. He checked plumbing and electricity. She admired the gables, the porch details, the intricate inlaid wood floors, the landscaping. "I think so."

"There's plenty of room," he added more seriously, opening the passenger's door for her. "Joe will have a bigger room than the closet he's stuck in now."

Gillian had to admit Joe's room was small. She said nothing, but smiled. She'd assessed everything accurately. Alex grumbled about Joe, but one of his primary concerns was Joe's comfort and happiness now.

"I suppose it sounds dumb to be this excited about a building, especially for someone who has traveled everywhere."

"So have you." As he touched her back, she felt a quick jolt of pleasure. She tried to remember when she'd been excited lately. She'd been thrilled to get the job offer in Hawaii, but real excitement? The last time she'd felt it had been when he'd kissed her.

"The difference is you wanted to travel," he said while sliding in behind the steering wheel. "You did a lot of it willingly when you were working as a courier."

She remembered well those weekly trips to Japan while she'd been working for a computer corporation.

"Globe-trotting suits you."

She'd always wanted adventures, a chance to sample new experiences. And she'd been to places more beautiful than the college town where he and Shelby lived. Yet, she felt so content here, more content than she'd ever been anywhere.

Strange thinking, she reflected. To dodge more of it, for the next few hours she buried herself deliberately in the paperback while they drove the pine-lined highway. The gypsy flavor of *Carmen* flowed out from the CD player. The music relaxed her; concentrating on the story distracted her.

"We're almost there." When he slowed the Bronco, she looked up, saw they'd reached the edge of town. "I'm going to stop there," Alex said, pointing at a gas station. "I'll ask for directions to Mrs. Nevins's street."

He surprised her. In the past he had rarely asked for directions. That he planned to do so now indicated how sensitive he was to her anxiety. It wouldn't help her one bit if they got lost. She rolled down her window, letting the cool mountain breeze flutter across her face.

"We're near," he said, sliding back in.

Her stomach somersaulted. What if she learned where Lenore was and she refused to see her? What if she resolved nothing on this trip?

"Mockingbird Lane, 412."

She sat quietly while he negotiated the SUV down a tree-lined street. Bungalows lined it.

"There it is."

Gillian stared where he'd pointed. Tension knotted muscles in her shoulders. Another uncertainty slammed at her. What if this was a mistake?

"Gillian, come on," Alex urged. He'd opened her door, stood beside her, his hand out.

She gripped it, needed his support more than she'd anticipated. While they strolled up the walkway, she tried to remember that the woman had agreed to see her. Even before they reached the porch, the door opened.

A plump woman with tightly curled white hair, pale blue eyes and a quick smile greeted them. At the moment she looked troubled. Mildred Nevins claimed she'd been expecting their visit since Alex's phone call to her yesterday. But she stood at the opened door for so long that Gillian believed she might shut it on them. "Come in," she finally said.

Gillian tightened her grip on Alex's hand. She wasn't looking for a sister or brother. The baby had died. What if Rachel and Sean were right? They believed nothing would be gained by talking to Lenore.

Mildred, walking ahead of them with a cane, led them onto a terrace with a view of the woods. "It's nice out here. Why don't you sit down." She gestured toward the white wrought-iron chairs with blue cushions. "Tell me what you need?"

"Your help." Gillian rushed words. "I really need your help."

"Mr. Hunter explained your situation." She looked from Alex to her. "But anything I know is hearsay."

Hungry for information, Gillian offered an assurance. "That's all right. It will still be more than I know now."

Slowly she settled on a chair across the white patio table from them and hooked her cane on the arm of the chair. "What is it that you want to know?"

"I'm sure Alex told you that I'm trying to find Lenore Selton."

"I didn't," Alex cut in. "I told her we were interested in locating Edith."

"Yes, that's true." Of course, he'd follow a logical procession and go A to B to get to C. "I want to find her."

The woman looked even more distressed. "Are you acquainted with Edith and Lenore?"

Gillian had to be honest. "No, I don't know them."

"Oh." What Gillian interpreted as relief entered the woman's eyes. "Then, it's easier to tell you this." Her gaze darted to Alex leaning back in his chair. "Lenore is no longer alive. Edith, her sister, was my friend. Well, you know that. Edith was still working at the university when it happened. She left for a short time to handle the funeral. This was five, perhaps six years ago."

All the questions Gillian had wanted to ask would never be answered. Disappointment descended on her. She'd hoped to meet Lenore, talk to her, try to learn if her father really had turned to her. Now what? She could only hope that Mildred had some answers. "Lenore had a baby, didn't she?"

"Oh, yes, Edith—"

"What about the father of the baby?" Gillian asked. "Did she ever mention him?"

"Well, he and Lenore weren't married, you know." She looked displeased by her own thought. "I understand he was already married. Edith thought that was terrible. You know, that her sister was seeing a married man."

Gillian didn't want to hear more. If she walked away now, she wouldn't have to face what she sensed was the truth, she wouldn't learn more. If she stayed, the woman might say something that would confirm what she wanted so badly to deny—her father really had had an affair, another daughter.

Tense, she sat straighter on the edge of the cushioned chair. Peripherally she saw Alex watching her closely. Did he know she was afraid? Could he tell she wanted to run as much as she wanted answers? She couldn't run. She'd come here to get the truth. "Do you know anything about that man?" she made herself ask. "Do you know his first name?" *Please, don't say my father's name, don't say Alan.* She asked Mildred the question, but her attention shifted to Alex, who'd angled himself toward her as if trying to get close before she heard something hurtful. At the moment she wished for his arms around her.

"I don't know his full name, but Edith mentioned his first name—Alan. Lenore met him at the school where they'd both taught."

Her chest hurt. Something physically was hurting her. Gillian touched her chest, wished she could rub away the ache. Her father had been the most perfect man in the world to her. He would never do that, she wanted to yell, but she kept quiet. There was no reason for this woman to lie, was there? No, but she might only be repeating what she believed. There was no real proof, and since Lenore's daughter died, there might never be any.

"You do understand," Mildred emphasized. "I didn't know Lenore, only Edith. But I know she was thrilled to have Lenore and her baby with her even if it was only for a little while."

A second passed. Then two. Alex's hand tightened on hers. Slowly Gillian slanted a look at the woman. "What did you say?"

"Well, Lenore didn't stay long. Edith really felt bad when her sister and her baby left for California."

What was this woman talking about? According to the diary, the baby had died. This made no sense. Gillian shook her head. "No. You're wrong. You must have misunderstood. Did you ever meet Lenore?"

"Actually, no, I didn't."

"Then you're wrong," Gillian said firmly.

The woman raised a baffled look at her. "About what, dear?"

"The baby. There was no baby. Lenore's daughter died."

Puzzlement deepened the lines of age in Mildred's face. "Oh, but that's not true. You're mistaken. The child—Carly, yes, that's her name, she's alive. Like I was going to say, Edith adored her niece whenever she went to visit. Frankly I thought she was more of a mother to Carly than Lenore was."

"Please—I don't understand." She needed to find Edith. Lenore's sister would clear this up. After all, this child had been her niece. It was possible that Mildred was talking about another daughter. Lenore could have had more than one child, one daughter.

"Do you know where Edith is now?" Alex asked as if sensing how muddled she felt.

"When Edith retired," Mildred went on, "she moved to Silver Creek because Lenore's daughter was living there then. I can give you directions and an address." Mildred started to inch forward on her chair. "You see, that's how I knew about Lenore's daughter. She's the reason Edith moved. Carly wanted to leave California and came here. Of course, it's possible neither of them is there now," Mildred said.

Gillian zeroed in on the woman again. "Why do you say that?"

"Because during a phone call a year ago, Edith told me that Lenore's daughter had been moving around a lot lately. I don't know why she did that, but Edith was pleased to have her so near for a change. I'm afraid I don't know much more."

When she drew a map to Edith's house, Gillian stood to leave. "About how old is this—Carly?"

"I believe she'd be around your age. I never met her, but Edith spoke so highly of her niece," Mildred said while moving with them to the door. "She was bright but didn't have a wonderful life probably because of her mother. Lenore always wanted what she couldn't have, and moved them a lot. That was all I recall Edith saying."

Gillian squeezed the woman's hand. "Thank you. I appreciate your time." She gave her the best smile she could produce, but she felt weak-kneed as she stepped outside with Alex.

The moment they hit the air, his arm came around her shoulder. "Gillian, lean on me."

"Oh, God, Alex." Her legs felt weak. "I can't believe this."

Chapter Eight

He wished he could make this easier. The woman had dropped a bomb.

While they moved toward his Bronco, she sank against him. "I thought there was no child anymore," she said unevenly. "If Mildred is right, there's a person out there who might be family. A sister."

Keeping her in the crook of his arm, Alex walked stride for stride with her to his SUV. None of this could be easy. And he knew her well enough to guess she was mentally challenging everything she'd learned. Because he assumed she needed quiet time, he left her alone with her thoughts during the drive home. She was hurting, he concluded. She might not admit it, but he knew she'd placed her father on a pedestal, believed he could do no wrong. Alex glanced her way, read the sorrow in her face. Memories had been tarnished. Alex could have warned her; he knew that fathers weren't perfect. Some of them didn't even give a damn.

With unseeing eyes Gillian stared out the window at the blur of passing scenery. Mildred had to be wrong. Shock, disbelief, a dozen emotions had burrowed within her since the woman had said those words.

Carly.

Was it possible the woman who might be their sister hadn't died? Why would their mother lie about that in her diary? If she wanted to adopt the child, she wouldn't. More likely, Lenore had lied, told their mother that the baby had died. But why would she?

Her only hope was to talk to Edith and get answers. In the meantime, she had to call Rachel and Sean. How would her sister and brother react to the news? Like her, would they tend not to believe any of this? How could they without proof?

"It's dinnertime. Do you want to stop somewhere?"

It took a moment for Alex's words to register. "Yes, okay." She could barely think about anything except what she'd learned from Mildred.

"Is that place all right?" he asked, directing her attention to a local steakhouse, a rustic-looking place with a plank wrap-around porch and horseshoe handles on the entrance doors.

Gillian nodded, not sure she'd be able to eat.

"Gillian, we could go home."

That wasn't really fair to him, she reminded herself. He was probably starving. "No, we need to eat." She would manage dinner. And more. Her best trait was to deal with frustrations, to bounce back from disappointments. At least, Rachel said so. Gillian hoped her sister had pegged her accurately. And for a while, she wanted to think about other people. Deliberately she avoided talking about their visit to Mildred. "When will Joe be home?" she asked after they were seated in the restaurant.

"Tomorrow evening."

She scanned the interior, the sawdust sprinkled over the plank floors, the dark wood walls, the decorative touches of miniature covered wagons, of hanging Tiffany lamps. "You haven't said. When Joe called yesterday," she said, remembering his phone call, "did he talk about the reunion?"

"He said he was having a good time." Over a glass of beer, Alex made a face. "Not much more."

How sad that they didn't really talk. He was so fortunate to still have his father. She wished—she wished hers was alive. He would tell her that this was all a mistake. "I'll have to move out of his room in the morning."

Reaching across the table, he suddenly curled his hand around hers. Since the kiss, his touch meant even more to her. "He'll stay with Loretta for a while."

At the unexpected contact, Gillian shook her head. If he was too tender, if he showed too much sympathy, she would lose control of her emotions in the middle of the restaurant. "Don't be too nice," she appealed.

He looked pained. "Nice?"

So easily he made her smile. He could always do that. "Nice is sexy," she assured him.

"And I'm...?"

Despite her disturbed thoughts, a laugh rose in her throat. "You're fishing for a compliment." Her fingers squeezed his with a silent message, a thank-you for trying to help her forget about all she'd learned—at least for a short time. "And you're nice." What woman wouldn't be attracted to tall, dark and handsome? "Very nice, Professor."

His thumb stroked the inside of her wrist. "I'm glad you didn't say it meant boring."

"Never boring."

The music, a dreamy country song about one more dance, brought couples to the small dance floor. She looked up to find Alex standing beside her. "Come on," he said, holding out a hand.

She knew he wasn't crazy about dancing. On a laugh, she stood, took his hand. She stopped laughing when he gathered her in his arms. She felt as if she belonged there. Her cheek resting against his, she curled her hand around his neck and closed her eyes. She went with the sensation. "We've never done this before," she murmured, too aware of the heat from him.

In a slow, seductive caress, he stroked her back. "Guess it was time."

Was he talking about the dance or the kiss? Heat churned within her. She was conscious of everything:

the warmth of the strong hand at the small of her back, the hard thighs brushing against hers, the light breath fanning her ear. With his body close, swaying with hers, he took her away from everything that had happened earlier. She hadn't expected to feel like smiling or laughing. She hadn't expected to feel so much. It was all because of him.

She enjoyed the dance, dinner and conversation. Most of all, he'd made her forget for a little while. "Thank you," she said later after her last bite of steak.

From across the table his gaze met hers. "The food was good."

"For everything," she said meaningfully. "And I was hungrier than I thought. But then, I've never had a problem with eating."

"I remember." He grinned. "I remember now a night at your apartment. All you had were pickles and bread. A person who eats pickle sandwiches will eat anything."

Like a lifeline she seized his tease. "I was hungry." Actually she'd thought the sandwich was awful, but after she'd toasted the bread, she'd reached for the jar of pickles to read the label, and he'd made a comment, assuming she'd planned to have some on her toast. That had been as good as a dare. Five years ago she'd never walked away from any kind of dare. More mature now she was less inclined to take risks, do something just to prove she would. It occurred to her that he still saw her as that impetuous, flighty girl he'd met in class one breezy autumn day. "I've changed,'' she said, speaking her thought as he read the bill.

He raised his eyes from his opened wallet.

"I wouldn't do that today," she said, standing with him while he placed money on the table. "I wouldn't do something just to prove a point." But hadn't she been striving to keep everything casual between them, to convince herself that her feelings hadn't changed for him?

He sent her a quick look, no more, when they climbed into his Bronco. "Isn't the search for Lenore to prove something?"

She had to admit that was partially true. She hadn't wanted to believe her father had broken a marriage vow. That Lenore's daughter was alive meant nothing. They didn't know if Lenore had lied or if her baby was a Quinn.

Oh, stop it, Gillian. Mildred, who had no reason to lie, had confirmed that Lenore had an affair with a man named Alan. If everyone else could accept that, why was she having such a hard time with it?

The question nagged at her during the drive home. Lost in thought when Alex switched off the ignition, she looked up, surprised to see they were at Loretta's.

Gillian opened the passenger door. Try as she might, she couldn't stifle her anger. Her mother had indicated that her father was disgusted with himself for being unfaithful, but that didn't change the outcome. "Why?" she murmured, speaking her thought.

"Why what?" Alex asked, slipping his fingers on her arm as they walked toward the door.

"There are couples who want children and go for years trying to have them, and then there's my father. Something he wished had never happened resulted in a child." Immediately she shook her head. "No, that's not true. He wanted the child. I'm sure he did."

When they returned to Alex's apartment, Gillian hadn't shaken away her ambivalence.

She had been wavering, one minute denying that anything had happened and the next minute trying to drum up reasons or excuses for why it had all happened. While she talked to Rachel, she reined in her frustrations about having no firm answers regarding Carly. But when she repeated everything she'd learned to Sean, her voice broke.

"What the hell is going on?" His shock rippled through to her. "Why would Mom write that the baby had died if it hadn't? She'd planned to adopt it," he said about their mother. "Isn't that what Rachel told us she read in Mom's diary?"

At first Rachel, too, had refused to believe any of it. After all, she'd been the one who'd read the diary, seen the entry in their mother's handwriting that the baby had died.

"All you have is this woman's word for it that she—Carly—is alive," Sean finally said.

"I know. That's what Rachel said, too. I have to go to Silver Creek and see if she's living there."

"You know it's possible this is someone pretending to be Lenore's daughter. This Mildred Nevins said Lenore and her child had moved away. How could her aunt, Edith Selton, be sure it's the same child?''

''According to Mildred she didn't die at birth,'' Gillian reminded him, and realized he, too, wanted to resist this.

''Never mind,'' he said in a resigned tone. ''I'm making no sense. They didn't come looking for us. We went looking for them. Why would they be trying to scam us?''

Sean had become financially well-off. So had Rachel since marrying Kane. His charter boat business of two boats had grown into four, the result of word-of-mouth advertising by the populace of Hubbard Bay where they lived, a form of restitution for treating him unfairly for years because of a misconception. But Carly might not even know about them.

''Do you want me to come? You don't have to do this alone.''

''I'm all right.'' She shifted on the sofa, tucking her legs beneath her. ''Alex is here. He'll go with me.''

''You sound positive of that.''

Her fingers cramping from holding the phone too tightly, she transferred it to her other ear. ''He said he would.''

''He's a good friend.''

''Yes.'' *A good friend.*

''Not more?''

Why would he ask that? ''Of course not.'' Had she said Alex's name in the way of a lover? That was absurd, she countered. They weren't lovers. One kiss was all they'd shared. With an ''I love you,'' she said goodbye to her brother. If he'd asked more, what would she have said?

She couldn't lie. Alex was more than a friend now. Turning, she saw him standing with his shoulder braced against the doorjamb. "They're stunned. We all agree that I should go to Silver Creek."

He came near and set a cup of coffee on the oak coffee table. "We can go tomorrow."

"No, tomorrow Joe comes home. You should be here."

"Gillian, if we don't go tomorrow——"

"I know." As his fingertips caught her chin, warmth spread through her. "But you told me Grant invited us to his house for a barbecue tomorrow night," she said, recalling how much Shelby was looking forward to it. "And the following day Shelby starts school, so you have to be here."

"That's right."

As anxious as she was to learn the truth, she didn't want to go alone. "It's okay, Alex. I can wait a few more days." She avoided his stare. *Coward,* her own mind screamed.

"Tell me about the phone calls." He brushed strands of hair away from her cheeks. "What else did your brother and sister say?"

"Even before this, Rachel believed the baby in the diary was our half sister. And Sean——I'm not sure. He's so wary, but I know he accepts that Dad was unfaithful."

"That's what they feel." He settled on the cushion near her. "What about you? You still aren't sure?"

She'd been numb ever since she'd heard Mildred's

words. "I'm trying to accept all of it." She'd been feeling mean-spirited, naive. Who was she to judge what happened decades ago? "If Carly is alive—if she is our sister, then she deserves what we had." The memories. Wonderful memories. "She never knew Dad. If she really is his child, she deserves to know about him, to know he was good and kind, and I believe didn't know she survived."

Sympathy shadowed his eyes. "She might have her own feelings of abandonment because she never knew her father."

Who would understand that better than him? "Yes, I guess that's possible. And that's not fair. He didn't abandon her. He didn't even know about her."

"You're wrong about something." He smiled. "You told me that you've changed. But you haven't." He draped an arm behind her, toyed with a strand of her hair. "You always had a tender heart."

"We've both changed, Alex." She strove to think about anything except the latest family revelation.

"I'd like to believe I'm not such a stick-in-the-mud anymore. No one could live with Shelby and take himself too seriously," he added. "And then there was you."

"Me...?" Lightly with his knuckles he stroked her cheek. Whether or not he meant to, he quickened her pulse. "How did I change you?" she asked, trying to sound calmer than she felt.

"You forced me to laugh at myself, especially when I wasn't your favorite person."

Unable to look away, she stared at his smiling

mouth. "When I first met you, you were so inflexible, so serious. It took me months to get past my first impression and see that a sense of humor existed beneath that. I remember the exact moment that I knew we could be friends."

"When?"

That question made her smile. She liked the idea that she'd aroused his curiosity. He was a man of great control. It was fun to see him baffled or simply giving in to a spontaneous emotion like cracking up with laughter.

"When?" he repeated.

"When we were on that dig, it had rained, poured, actually. You were plodding up a hill of mud when your feet slipped."

"And slid down on my belly, face in the mud."

"And you laughed."

"You did, too, when you came tumbling down right behind me."

She remembered more. At the bottom of the hill, mud-coated, he'd sat up, laughing. So was she when he'd pulled her up. She'd laughed so hard that she'd collapsed against him. "I never expected you to laugh."

"I never expected you to hug me."

"I thought I couldn't stand you," she admitted. She knew then that she liked him. How simple it sounded. How complicated feelings suddenly were.

They'd always been honest with each other. If she told him what she was feeling, maybe he'd say something to make her laugh and she'd stop making too much of everything between them. "When I talked to Sean, he wondered about us being involved."

She'd thought he would laugh at that, or at least smile. Instead he looked so serious. "Is it so difficult for you to consider the idea?"

"Have you ever thought about...*us?*" She sounded breathy even to her own ears.

"I'm not blind. Of course I have." He fingered a strand of hair near her cheek. "You're beautiful. You dazzle a man."

He made her heart quicken. Emotion filling her, she sighed as he slipped a hand behind her neck. "This is crazy, isn't it?"

"Why is it?" Alex believed they couldn't keep ignoring this. He wanted to hold her again, feel the soft contours of her body. He wanted to kiss her. Make love with her. She kept staring at him with eyes that appeared larger. Greener. Even more seductive than usual. She was so beautiful. He'd always thought she was one of the most beautiful women he'd ever seen.

Ever since they'd gotten home, he'd wanted to draw her into his arms. Dozens of other times he'd touched her, but something was different this time. Why? Because she'd truly needed him? She never had before. Independent to a fault, she'd always seemed capable of handling anything. She would handle this, too, he knew. She was a strong, resilient woman. But he wanted to be part of this, to be the one she could lean on if she needed someone.

He didn't know what to call what he was feeling for her. Or why it had happened. They'd been together too many times to count, during the past five years, and never before had he felt this pull, something magnetic, magical—something impossible to resist.

Absolutely they were all wrong for each other. They were supposed to be good buddies, nothing else. They'd never have a future together. She couldn't stay still very long. He couldn't deal with another move. He'd known too many in his youth. Yet he wanted her. He wanted her as he'd wanted no other woman. ''Tell me what you want? What you really want.''

Her eyes not leaving his, she brushed her fingers along his cheek. ''You.''

With one whispered word she shattered every thought in his brain. He lowered his head. Even before he closed his mouth over hers, she pressed against him. For days he'd imagined holding her like this, kissing her. None of those fantasies compared to this. She filled his mind with her sweetness.

Thinking came secondary suddenly. When he backed her against the wall, their bodies came together hard. She curled her fingers in his shirtfront. He ran a hand down her hip to her thigh. Their mouths clung as if hunger, sudden and voracious, had attacked them, and they would never get enough of each other.

He'd never felt this. Never. It seemed so dumb. He was thirty-two years old. He'd known passion. He'd felt the heat curling through him. But never had he known this raw impatience. He'd been trying to fill his life with someone. Friends had sent women his way, intelligent, lovely women, women who shared his interests, women who should have been his perfect match. And no one had mattered, not like this. And he wasn't even sure what "this" was. As strong and solid as their friendship was, this was something fragile, too delicate to test, for fear it would break.

With a low oath he lifted his mouth from hers, stared into eyes dark with desire. How could he explain what she was doing to him, making him feel? She looked flushed, her lips swollen from his kiss. It didn't matter that he should back away, take his hands off her. Unable to resist, he softly kissed her throat. "I don't know how this happened. Or why."

Gillian forced eyes open, and with effort she clawed her way back from some dreamy, intoxicating place. For a while thinking hadn't existed. She'd simply wanted to go with the emotion.

"Stay with me," he said.

She couldn't speak. She could barely breathe.

His strong hands, gentle hands, held her face still. "I want you. I want you so badly I'm aching. Maybe you don't want me to say that but—"

"I do," she cut in. "Alex, I do." Taking chances came easier for her than him, she reasoned. One of them had to be bold. She wanted this. He needed to know just how much. She melted against him. "But we won't expect anything." She needed that assurance, she knew. "Promise me," she insisted.

"I promise," he said on a whisper.

Only then did she close her eyes again.

Clinging, she buried her face in his neck, felt him

lifting her, gathering her in his arms. She'd never expected him to carry her. She'd never expected him to feel this way about her.

In the bedroom's faint light his eyes met hers when he let her feet touch the floor. A wordless plea whispered on the air between them. *Don't let this be a mistake.* How could it be? she wondered, when it felt so right to be in his arms, to have his mouth on hers.

In silence she ran her hands over his back, tugged his shirt from his jeans to inch her fingers beneath it, to feel sleek, masculine flesh.

With a slowness that rushed warmth through her, he tugged her T-shirt over her head. Then the chill of the evening danced across her skin as he slipped one thin strap of her bra and then the other off her shoulders. She felt no self-consciousness. It felt so right to be here with him.

Beneath the moonlight filtering in, she saw longing in his eyes—for her. Even more certain that this was where she should be, she brought her mouth to his again. Briefly she wondered how they'd waited this long. With the taste of him on her lips, she yanked at buttons on his shirt. Trembling fingers touched sinewy skin. Muscles rippled beneath her fingertips.

Then his palms were on her hips, urging down her jeans. She closed her eyes, obeyed each subtle command of his hands, absorbed the touch of them inching down her panties, caressing her hips, her thighs.

Softly she moaned when he kissed her stomach, each breast. He murmured something, then lowered her to the bed. Words didn't matter. She looked up, watched him free himself of the rest of his clothes, and she waited, aching. The second flesh met flesh, she couldn't stop touching. In a memorizing manner, as they faced each other, she stroked the sturdy hardness of his chest, the taut flesh at his hip, the thin line of hair at his navel. She felt him quiver, accepted the power he was willingly giving her.

Then, head back, she gave his mouth freedom to explore. Sensation hummed through her when he lowered his head, when his tongue grazed her nipple. On a moan she squeezed her eyes tight. He made her forget, made her world shift. With a skilled caress, with a stroke of his tongue, he took her breath away.

His mouth and tongue coursed a trail from one breast to the other. Her skin tingled as his tongue moistened a nipple again. Wild, she gave in to his strong hands. Never had she imagined him like this—bold and wild and exciting. Never had she expected this yearning.

When he filled himself with her, madness swept through her. She wanted to catch her breath, needed to, but was almost beyond thinking with each hot breath searing her flesh. "Alex, please."

She didn't have to beg, Alex could have told her. He would give her anything she wanted. Give. Pleasure. That was all he cared about. He tasted, seduced. He craved. He'd always been a patient man, a disciplined one. But she made him senseless. Even as he sought every inch of her, as he rode on her pleasure, sensation wrenched his gut, made him as bewildered as if he was in a drunken stupor. The need, the yearning filled him. She was so delicate, so strong. She was his friend—now his lover.

Bracing himself above her, he met her stare, saw the smile in her eyes as she arched up to meet him, and he reached into the bedside table for protection. On a low moan, throbbing, he slipped into her. His face inches above her, for a long moment he didn't move. He wanted to feel, just feel.

Eyes, soft and enticing, stared up at him, and a small smile played across her lips. Then they strained against each other, their skin damp, slick with heat's passion. They challenged. They blended. Heat bathed them, consumed them. Alex buried his face in her neck, closed his eyes, gave in. A shudder ripped through him. Light burst in his head. And his world was her.

Only her.

Chapter Nine

He awoke thinking of her. Years had passed since he awoke thinking of any female but his daughter. Lying in a jumble of sheets, he kept his eyes shut and wanted to go with his senses, to feel more than think. With a shift of his head on the pillow, he felt the heat of the morning sun. He knew she'd left his side. If he stretched out his hand, his fingers wouldn't caress her softness, the silky texture of her skin. He would never regret last night, but he needed to keep everything simple between them.

Turning his face into the pillow, he absorbed her scent on the pillowcase. It would haunt him as would every second he'd had with her last night. He shifted, rolled to the edge of the mattress but didn't sit up. After she'd left, he'd yearned for her in a way he'd desired no other woman. Never had he felt as if any of them had become a part of him, except when he'd been with Nicki. Only then. And now. Oh, God, he couldn't be in love with Gillian. He'd wreck everything between them. He didn't want to be in love.

"Open your eyes. I came to see if you were still sleeping. You're playing possum, aren't you?"

It took effort not to smile, not to pull her down, bury his face in her hair, in her scent. Her breath fluttered across his face, and a plan came to mind. He waited until she was poised over him, then caught her at the small of the back and yanked her down.

Startled, she squeaked. "Alex!" Laughing, she collapsed on top of him. "You sneak."

"Guilty." A hand on her backside, he flattened her against him.

"You keep surprising me."

He stared into green eyes dancing with good humor. "Is that good...or bad?"

"Hmm. Good. But—"

He kissed her to silence her next words. He didn't want them to talk about what had happened, to spoil the moment. Just feel, he wanted to say. "Let's not analyze this."

He felt the mouth against his smile. "That's the strangest thing you've ever said."

It probably was. But he didn't want to think too much. He didn't want to hear regret in her voice. He wanted to go with this moment. Sure it was head-in-the-sand thinking. But it was a safe way to hold on to what he'd found with her last night.

* * *

Content, mellow, Gillian lounged in a kitchen chair and soaked up the warm morning sunshine streaming through the slats of the blinds. From the bathroom Alex bellowed out an aria from *Rigoletto* over the rush of water in the shower. Behind her the coffee brewer hissed with the final drips. Wondering if Loretta wanted to drive with them to the airport to meet Joe that night, she prodded herself from a lazy mood and stretched for the phone.

With her question Loretta shared a surprise. Joe had called. She was on her way to the airport to pick him up. Promising not to tell Alex, excited for him, Gillian told Loretta about the house.

"Joe will be glad to hear that Alex has found something he likes. He knows Alex isn't happy about how cramped they are. Sometimes—" Loretta went quiet for a second. "He told me that he wishes he didn't have to impose on Alex, but the doctor did advise him to live with someone because of his heart condition."

"I know. I really believe they need to be together."

A smile came into Loretta's voice. "So do I."

Gillian hung up. She truly liked the woman and hoped Joe was genuinely fond of her, she realized. No longer hearing Pavarotti's rival, she removed fixings for an omelet and hurriedly chopped onions and tomatoes. She felt no strangeness being here, no strained morning-after discomfort.

Had she always had feelings for Alex? Last night, breathless, her skin damp with passion, she'd listened to his breathing, placed her hand on his chest to feel the beat of his heart, and she couldn't remember feeling happier. In the dreamy aftermath of their lovemaking, she'd wondered if this was where she belonged.

Beneath moonlight, in a lover's arms, it was easy to make too much of such moments, she knew, but how could she ignore the feelings that were hammering at her now with sunlight bathing her skin? She wanted to believe this could work. Most of all, she didn't want to lose what she'd had for years with him.

She moved to the refrigerator, flung open the door and smiled as she reached for the eggs from one of the well-stocked, organized shelves. In her apartment she'd had three staples: sugared corn flakes, a package of chocolate-chip cookies and bottled water. She grabbed the eggs, started the omelets and sipped another cup of coffee. Back at the refrigerator, she found four different kinds of cheese.

"Can't find what you're looking for?" he said suddenly close to her ear, and slowly slid an arm across her belly.

She sighed. "There's too much to choose from."

"I'll throw some of it away," he muttered against the side of her neck. "Let's have breakfast later."

She went with the moment, closed her eyes, yearned to give him anything he wanted for a little while longer.

An hour later, they were back in the kitchen when Joe opened the door.

A duffel bag in his hand, he narrowed his eyes at

them. "Something's different here," he said instead of a hello.

His arm on her waist, Alex scowled at him. "What are you doing here?"

"I called, told you I was coming home today."

"Yeah." His frown in place, he checked his watch. "Tonight. I was supposed to pick you up tonight."

Gillian didn't doubt his sour mood was because his plans for them to have the day together had been ruined. Discreetly she elbowed his rib, hoping he'd stop acting so surly. If he didn't, Joe was astute enough to guess what was different.

"Alex has news," she announced.

Joe stepped farther into the room. "What's that?"

"I found a house." Alex bent over the counter to scribble the address on a pad of paper. "I'll give you the address, and you can take a look at it. Tell me what you think."

"You're paying for it. You decide."

Gillian groaned. Why was he so brusque with Alex all the time?

With more effort than necessary, Alex ripped the paper from the pad. "Look at it," he said tersely and set the paper on the counter.

Gillian wanted to knock their heads together. *Say hi. How are you? How was your trip? Are you okay? I missed you.* Neither of them said the words.

"Loretta and I drove by the house on the way here from the airport."

Why hadn't Joe said that in the first place? Because Alex didn't respond, Gillian filled the silence.

"I told Loretta, gave her the address. I'm sorry if I ruined your surprise," she said to Alex.

"That's all right," he answered. "It's no big deal."

But the house was important to him. It represented all he'd felt cheated out of when he was a child. A place to belong mattered to him. She watched him step out of the room. He was usually such an open-minded man, so willing to meet people halfway. Everyone except his father.

"I'll put this away in a minute," Joe said about his duffel bag. "Did he tell you that I'll be staying at Loretta's for a while?"

"Yes." With disdain, she eyed the dried-out omelet in the pan and turned off the stove burner. "Joe, if you want, I can…"

"This will be fine." His grin more than his words convinced her. "If Alex asks, he'll find me at the nearby seniors' club today. He has the phone number."

Gillian wondered if he realized that it was because of Alex's ties to the community that Joe had a home, neighbors, a sense of fitting in. Did he really look down on Alex's choice of profession, his lifestyle? Why hadn't he ever told Alex he'd done well? "Did you know Alex could head an expedition to Turkey?"

Unzipping his duffel bag, Joe took a second before looking up.

Gillian thought she read surprise, and something more—maybe pride—in his eyes. "That's quite an honor," she said, wanting Joe to acknowledge what a success his son was.

"He won't be able to go," he said absently while he removed a small stuffed animal from his bag.

Gillian noticed it was a black-and-white whale that he'd obviously bought for Shelby.

"He needs to be around for his family," Joe commented.

A noise behind her shifted her attention from the immaculately folded shirts in Joe's bag to the doorway, where Alex stood with a shoulder braced against the frame.

No softness warmed his eyes. "Like *you* always were," he said.

The words were meant as criticism. Joe didn't respond, didn't have to. Such sadness clouded his eyes.

Gillian felt torn, wanting to reach out to him, yet understanding why Alex had said that and wanting to be loyal to him. "The house that Alex found is close to Loretta's," she said to break the silence and to incite some excitement from him. "And it's a charming house."

If only he would indicate that he liked the home his son had chosen.

Alex didn't give him a chance. Clearly he'd looked for his father to be pleased, and was hurt by Joe's noncommittal manner. "If you don't like it, say so."

Displeasure snapped in his father's eyes. "Did I say that?"

"Hell." Alex spun away. "You never say anything."

Gillian wanted to scream. They were both too proud. When Alex disappeared out the back door, she hurried toward it.

"Tell him—" Joe froze her at the open door with two words.

"Tell him what?" she asked, facing him.

"Tell him that I like it," he said, and turned away.

Why didn't you? She stared at his back, wanted to scream. Was the wall between them so impenetrable? Not waiting another moment, she took off after Alex.

When she got outside, he was nowhere in sight. Assuming he'd turned the corner, she jumped into her car. She got lucky. She drove south and turned left, then saw him. He'd only walked a couple of blocks. Pulling up to the curb, she rolled down the window. "Are you going to keep walking?"

The length of his stride, the ramrod set of his back spoke volumes to her.

"If you are," she added, "I'd like to go along."

Though he slowed his stride, the scowl on his face remained. "I won't be great company."

"I'll take my chances." She waited for his eyes to lock with hers again, then deliberately winked. "How much for a morning quickie, sweetie?"

"A morning...?" His laugh rippled on the air. "You're something." Smiling now, he approached her car.

She played her part to the hilt, resting a forearm on the edge of the open window, keeping her tone casual and sultry. "Want a ride?" She held a hand out of the car, palm up. "It's going to rain."

"A quickie?"

She wanted him to know she meant her next words. Despite his teasing tone, hers was deadly serious. "Anything you need."

He came up to the window, leaned close until only inches separated their faces, until his breath fanned her face. "You. I need you," he whispered.

Going back to the apartment never entered Alex's mind. And a quick one in the car belonged to teenagers. They found a motel several blocks away with plenty of amenities, including a whirlpool tub. They stopped at a gift shop and bought candles.

He closed the drapes; she lit the candles.

By candlelight they made love slowly, cuddled for a long time in the bed, then slipped into the jacuzzi. With only the flickering light and the water lapping around them, for the first time in hours, Alex felt tension seeping out of him. "I needed to get out of there, away from him."

Gillian sensed this was more about annoyance with himself than Joe. Alex liked to be in control, always.

"Sorry. You didn't deserve any of that. That was lousy of me, especially after last night. You deserved a nice day."

"It is." She shifted in the water to face him, to straddle his lap, to feel the slick texture of his flesh close to hers. "I'm with you."

His hands slid up her bare back.

"He upset you," she said simply, feeling that he needed to talk about his relationship with Joe.

"He always does. He actually expects me to be

around if he needs me. He was never near when I needed him. Joe's like Nicki. He always viewed what I decided to do with my life as lacking excitement.'' A mirthless laugh entered his voice. ''Now he wants what he never gave my mother and me. He wants a home. He wants stability.''

She waited for a long moment to let his mood turn gentle again. ''Yes, he does. He told me that he likes the house, Alex.''

''He likes it?'' His fingers paused on a slick, silky thigh. ''He said so?''

''Yes.''

He gave his head a shake. ''Why couldn't he tell me?''

She snuggled closer, pressed her breasts into him. ''I don't know.''

On a sigh, he buried his face in her hair, nuzzled her wet neck. ''You're good for me.''

''We've always been good together,'' she reminded him. It annoyed her that it had taken them five years to realize how good.

That evening the barbecue at Grant's helped keep Shelby's anxiety about school at bay, but while watching Grant baste the spareribs with barbecue sauce, Alex searched for more distractions. He'd considered suggesting a movie tomorrow, an after-school treat.

''There's a concert tomorrow evening at the town square,'' Grant said after listening to his concern. He shoved a serving spoon into his wife's potato salad now that another colleague had volunteered to play chef.

Standing beneath the patio overhang, Alex looked inside where Gillian had joined Grant's wife in the kitchen. She blended well with the group gathered. Nicki had sat by herself, looking as if she wanted to be elsewhere whenever they'd gone to a gathering.

"She's lovely, Alex."

He swung his attention to Grant. "Yes, she is."

"And seems perfect for Shelby."

And me? he wondered. "What were you saying about a concert?"

"It's a children's concert."

The idea appealed to Alex. Shelby needed something different and new to look forward to. "I'm hoping if I keep her busy thinking about other things, she won't fret so much about school."

"I'd like to have problems like that one day."

"You will," Alex assured him, knowing Grant and Deanna would find a way to have a family.

"Where's your father? He could have come along."

"He's with a lady friend," Gillian said, appearing at their side with a bowl of coleslaw and a bean salad.

Grant responded with a smile. "He has more of a love life than you do," he gibed at Alex.

Alex caught Gillian's wink and felt a shaft of longing cut through him. A day ago that would have been true. But so much had changed. During passion, he didn't think about what was improbable. Yet there was no certainty they would know more of those quiet intimate moments, or the mindless passionate ones. He only knew that standing with her now, with friends and their families around them, he didn't want to let her out of his sight. And he wanted more: he wanted her standing side by side with him; he wanted to share troubles and joys with her. He wanted her in his life forever.

First-day-of-school nerves hit Shelby before she was out of bed the next morning. When she shuffled into the kitchen for breakfast and complained about a tummy ache, Alex geared up for a problem.

Before it grabbed hold, Joe came to the rescue. "You can't be sick. You have a big day planned." He'd wandered in at breakfast time, though he'd declined Alex's offer to make him pancakes. "School. Then a grown-up concert."

At the stove Alex glanced back over his shoulder at the two of them. Time with his granddaughter on her big day had obviously brought him upstairs. Alex accepted that they got along better than he and his father did. He'd heard that relationships were often better when one generation was skipped.

"And this morning before school, me and Gillian are going shopping for new clothes," Shelby said, brightening.

"You're going shopping, too?"

"Gillian suggested it," Alex said.

"That'll be fun."

It occurred to Alex that if he'd suggested the shopping trip, his father would have given it a thumbs-down on principle. A short trip to the store for school clothes before Shelby's afternoon kindergarten class had sounded like a good idea to Alex.

"Where's Gillian now?" Joe asked, breaking the silence.

"Showering." Alex ladled pancake batter into a frying pan. The urge to join her had hit him the moment he'd heard the running water. He'd been enjoying a honey of a fantasy before Joe had come in.

"Alex?" Over the rim of his glasses, Joe stared at him quizzically. "Are you listening? I said I've been spending time at the seniors' club lately, and they need help with some of the people. I'm thinking of volunteering there."

"Sounds good."

"I need to keep busy."

Alex made a guess that Shelby wasn't the only one jittery this morning. He glanced at the calendar, noted Joe had marked today on the calendar for his doctor's appointment. "What time do you go today? Nine-thirty?"

With the reminder, his scowl returned. "I'd better get ready," he said, standing. He drained the coffee in his cup, then bent down to Shelby. "You have fun today."

She stopped folding a napkin. "Okay, Grandpa."

"Call me. Tell me what happens," Alex requested, not certain Joe would.

He was slow to answer as if weighing his response. "I'll call."

"Bye, Grandpa." Shelby darted to him for a hug and kiss. "Daddy, know what?" she asked when the door closed behind Joe. "I've been thinking."

He flipped the pancakes, then gave her his full attention. "Is this important?"

"Uh-huh."

"Okay." He faced her with his best deadpan expression. They'd had a similar serious talk when she'd come to the conclusion that she would give a name to her favorite stuffed animal—the gorilla from Gillian. Leaning back against the counter, Alex sipped his coffee. "What do you want to tell me?"

"I think it would be okay if Gillian were my new mommy."

He held the coffee cup in midair. "You think..." *Talk fast. She's sharp.* He couldn't let her get her hopes up about something that wouldn't happen. "Honey, Gillian's a friend."

"But—" Her brows veed.

With her hesitation, Alex hunkered down to her level. "What do you want to say?" Clearly something had confused her.

"You kiss her like Jenna's mommy and daddy kiss."

"When did you see me...?"

"When she gave you a hamburger."

Yesterday at Grant's, when he'd done that, he'd thought no one had noticed. "Shelby, it's not that easy to get a mommy," he said, deciding to breeze over a discussion about the kiss.

"Why not?"

"Well—" Tough question. You can't order a mommy, he supposed he could say. You have to love her. Nope, that wouldn't work. She did love Gillian. She has to love us. Well, he knew she loved

Shelby, and in some way she loved him. But it couldn't be a brotherly and sisterly type. There had to be passion.

Standing, he turned away to hide his frown and shoved the spatula beneath a pancake. There was plenty of passion. He looked back, wondering how he would answer her question. He didn't need to, he realized.

With the attention span of a five-year-old, her head jerked toward the doorway when the theme music of her favorite television program wafted in to them.

Relieved, Alex said nothing as she jumped off her chair and flew toward the door. "I'll call when breakfast is ready," he yelled out to her. Sometimes it was best not to finish conversations.

"She's in a hurry."

Startled, he twisted around with a frown.

Gillian teasingly copied his expression. "Were you daydreaming, Professor?" Dressed in a pumpkin-colored pullover with a zipper and black jeans, she looked as carefree as one of his students. "Still are, it seems." Smiling, she crossed the white-and-gray tile floor. "About what, I wonder?"

Featherlight her lips brushed his. She could make him crawl if she wanted to, he realized at that moment and deepened the kiss. He'd missed being with a woman first thing in the morning, getting a kiss before breakfast.

"Good morning."

"I'd say so." She smelled sweet, soapy clean. He drew a long, deep breath to savor the scent. "Are you ready for your big day of shopping?"

Overhead lights gleamed on her hair. "Can't wait." Her soft laugh curled around him, aroused a memory of its soft, seductive sound in his ear during lovemaking. But more than the passion made him ache for her. She was so caring, so thoughtful. He knew that for his sake she'd put her own plans aside. "We should be able to take that drive to Silver Creek tomorrow."

"That'll be fine." Though smiling, she studied him with serious eyes. "But let's wait and see what happens with Joe."

Lightly, he kissed the tip of her nose. "Thanks for caring about Joe. But I know you want to go."

In what he viewed as her avoiding his stare, she looked down, toyed with the collar of his shirt. "Don't you know I'm using your problems to avoid my own?"

"Yes, I know." That might be true, but she possessed an enormous amount of thoughtfulness for others. The thank-you was deserved. "What's worrying you?"

"A woman I don't know." She sighed, seeming so uncertain. "I've tried not to think too much about meeting Carly, but what if she doesn't want to know us? What if she likes her life just the way it is? It's possible Carly has bad feelings about Dad. We don't know what Lenore told her about our father. She might have made it sound as if he'd abandoned her because she was pregnant."

"That might not be such a far-fetched idea."

"I don't believe that."

Alex would have liked to drop the subject. Distressing her wasn't his goal. Making her face the truth was. "Think about something else. What if your father only let your mother believe that they were going to adopt after she found out about the affair?" As a flash of anger flared in her eyes, he spoke quickly. "Hear me out," he appealed. "This might have more to do with your mother's problem. He might have been trying to offer her hope."

"By lying to her? Absolutely not. He wouldn't do that." Her voice trailed off. "You're thinking I don't really know him as well as I think, aren't you? Well, maybe I don't," she said, much calmer. "But I still don't believe he'd be that dishonest with her. And I don't know why my mother was led to believe the baby had died, but I don't think my father was part of that deception."

Alex loved her loyalty. She possessed a lot of admirable traits, but loyalty was her finest. When she believed in someone, she didn't waver.

"I'll prove that," she said firmly. "But at what price to a woman I don't know? Will I hurt Carly, spoil her memories of her mother, play havoc with her life? I don't want to hurt this woman."

Sometimes she astonished him, he realized. Instead of protecting herself, she was willing to meet this woman who might spoil memories she held dear, and she worried about that woman's feelings, not her own. "You know there's another possibility," he said.

She sighed. "I think I know what you're going to say. It's possible we won't like her. That's what Sean mentioned the last time I talked to him."

Alex wasn't surprised someone other than Gillian had thought of that. She tended to like everyone. "He's right." As she drew back, he reluctantly released her. "You may wish you'd never started this."

"I can't consider that. I need to know about her mother, about what she and my father felt. Only Carly and Edith can tell me that." She strolled to the cabinet for the maple syrup. "If it's okay with you, after breakfast I'll call Loretta and tell her that I'll watch Shelby. I was going to take her shopping later, but we can go now. I think Loretta would like to go with Joe today to the doctor's."

He turned off the warming oven. "Did she say so?"

Gillian noted the line deepening between his brows. Did the idea of Joe becoming involved with someone bother him? "She doesn't want him to be alone."

"Then it's good that she's going," he said, clarifying in her mind that this wasn't an adult child's problem about his father being with some woman other than his mother. "I couldn't go with him."

"I'm sure Loretta knew you'd have difficulty taking another day off."

"Gillian, you're sweet." Just a hint of regret hung in his voice. "But we both know that Joe wouldn't want me with him." His gaze strayed to the clock on the wall above the kitchen counter. "I have to leave soon. I'll get Shelby for breakfast."

"Okay." She ambled to the refrigerator to pour Shelby's milk. If only there was some way to get Alex and Joe talking.

Chapter Ten

After she and Alex and Shelby had breakfast, Gillian called Loretta. Relief flooded Loretta's voice when Gillian said she would watch Shelby. Clearly the woman had wanted to go with Joe to the doctor's.

"Call me," Gillian insisted to Alex before he left for the university. "Let me know what's happening with Joe." Only then did she realize how her words had sounded. Whether she planned to or not, she was becoming part of the family. Even when she wasn't with them, she thought about Alex and Shelby and Joe. She'd always been so certain about what she didn't want, and suddenly she wasn't sure of anything except how right it felt to be here with them.

"If he calls me," Alex responded on a parting note and a kiss meant to make her miss him.

She watched him leave, then strolled toward Shelby's room, worry for him shadowing her. What if Joe didn't call Alex? What if he refused to reach out to his son? She believed Joe didn't want their relationship this way, but felt so much guilt that he needed Alex to make the first move. One thing Joe would never admit to was fear. But in his own way, perhaps that's what he felt with Alex. He cared deeply but couldn't show it. And if he reached out to his son, and Alex rejected him, in Joe's mind, did that mean there would be no hope for them to get closer?

"Gillian, are we going to go now?" Shelby asked, bringing her back to her surroundings. In the center of the room, surrounded by doll clothes, Shelby was packing the clothes into the bright-pink doll suitcase.

"In a minute. Let's do your hair first." After Shelby sat on the edge of the bed, Gillian brushed her hair, fastened clips on strands near her ears. In a mirror she met the little one's eyes and leaned forward to rest her chin on top of her head. She was so sweet, Gillian thought. "Now we're leaving." Straightening, she backed up several steps, then reached for Shelby's small hand and took off at a run to stir her laughter.

They were only a step from the front door when the phone rang. "Don't answer it," Shelby appealed as Gillian halted and swung toward it.

"Shelby, I can't do that." She let go of her hand. "Could you?" she asked on the way to the phone.

"Daddy can." Her voice lowered. "That's what answering machines are for."

Gillian grinned at her impersonation of her father and reached for the receiver.

"Joe doesn't know anything," Alex told her after saying hello. "He has to go to a different location for a different test."

"That might not mean it's anything serious," she said, to offer some reassurance about the news to come.

"Gillian, to him everything is serious. He doesn't handle any kind of illness well. He can't figure out how any illness, including the common cold, would dare afflict him."

She wasn't surprised at his words. A man who spent so many years in the military would carry an abundance of pride and a macho attitude.

"How is Shelby?"

"She's fine," Gillian assured him. I miss you, she wanted to say, but would he want to hear those words?

"Good." She heard in his voice that he was pleased. "I'll be home in time to take her to school."

Alex was definitely one of the sandwich generation, bearing responsibility for a child and a parent. "On your lunch hour?"

"It works out perfectly."

"When do you eat?"

Amusement rang in his voice. "You're kidding."

A solution popped into her mind. "I'll drive Shelby to you. That will save you time."

Their trip to the store proved just enough distraction. Shelby asked Gillian three times if she liked her new butterfly hair clips. After leaving the store, they stopped at the apartment to hang up clothes and pick up lunch.

At eleven-thirty she and Shelby waited in the parking lot adjacent to Goldwater Hall at the university.

Craning her neck, Shelby spotted Alex first. "There's Daddy."

Dressed in khakis and a midnight-blue polo shirt, "Daddy" certainly drew his share of female looks, Gillian noted.

From the back seat, Shelby waved. "Daddy, Daddy!" The moment he opened the passenger door, she revealed part of the plan. "Gillian says you got to sit back here."

"I do?"

"'Cause she's driving."

"A chauffeur!" He spoke like it was a big deal, giving it dramatic flair for his daughter's benefit. "And how are you, m'lady?" he asked, joining his daughter in the back seat.

As expected, she giggled.

Gillian waited until he was settled, then reached back and handed him a brown bag. "And here."

"What's this?" Despite his question, he was already peering inside the bag.

"Lunch."

He pointed his nose at the contents of the bag. "Lunch?"

"*L-u-n-c-h.* The meal you always miss."

"I'll have to think of some way to thank you."

In the rearview mirror she met his stare, saw devilment in his eyes. "I'm sure you'll come up with something."

"She's still anxious," Alex said to her in a low voice. With his daughter's tiny hand gripped in his, he strolled beside her and Gillian toward the school gate.

"You'll both get through this," she said.

Gillian might find humor in this, but he was serious, full of misgivings, convinced Shelby would hate him for sending her off with strangers, for abandoning her. "I should have kept her home. What if some kid picks on her? What if her teacher does?" he whispered so Shelby wouldn't hear him.

"Alex, she'll be fine."

Of course she would be. She'd gone to preschool and had done fine. But preschool had been different. The class had been small, the teacher kind, the kids sweet. That he was being totally irrational didn't escape him.

"Daddy, there's Jenna. I gotta go."

At her tug on his hand, he hunkered down for a quick kiss.

"Can I go?"

"Go—" Before he could finish, she dashed off toward her friend.

Expecting Gillian's tease, he offered a warning while he stood. "Do *not* give me one of those I-told-you-so looks."

"Not me," she said lightly, and had the good grace to stifle a laugh.

* * *

That his daughter had left him without any qualms eased his mind. He found himself smiling when Gillian pulled into the university parking lot.

"See you later."

Shifting on the seat, he leaned toward her for a long, thorough kiss. "Later." He slid out of her rental car, not unaware of stares. He didn't care who saw him kissing her. In her own way she was indispensable to them. Alex doubted Gillian would be pleased to learn that. She'd made it a point not to have people depend on her. The truth was that none of them wanted her to do things for them, but each of them in their own way was beginning to rely on having her around. He couldn't help wondering, even hoping, that she'd have a hard time leaving.

But he knew it would be dumb to expect her to stick around. Why would she? She thrived on having a life that was a lot more exciting than a college professor could offer. To tell her what he felt wouldn't be fair to her. He didn't want her regretting the time with him or brooding that she might hurt Shelby or feeling obligated to stay with them.

With a shake of his head he wove a path to class. He considered all the complications suddenly in his life. And the worry. It shadowed him. Worry that Shelby would be less than thrilled with school after day one, worry that Gillian might get hurt by a woman named Carly, worry for Joe, especially now. All his life his father had been strong, invincible, and though Joe had never been around for him, Alex couldn't say Joe had been undependable. There had always been a roof over their heads, food on the table, even if Joe had been absent from their lives more than with them.

"Hi, Professor."

Alex focused on the girl in snug jeans, a bright-orange knit top and similar-colored hair. "Afternoon." He opened the door and let her precede him in.

His thoughts elsewhere, he struggled to keep his mind on a lecture about the sea people who attacked Egypt when Ramses II was in power. *Dull* described his lecture. Cursing his own preoccupation, he vowed he'd make it up to his students tomorrow.

At two o'clock he called the real estate agent, wanting to see the house again, then left for Shelby's school. It didn't matter that he was early. Patiently, eagerly he waited outside the school at the designated area where parents were allowed to gather. Was he the only one feeling as if the classroom doors would never open, that he'd never see his child again?

"I see you're early."

Startled, he swung around. At some moment Gillian had returned home and changed. She looked lovely in a snug, burgundy-colored top and long, flowered skirt.

"Sorry. I didn't mean to surprise you."

Glad to have her near, he slipped an arm around her waist. In fascination, he watched the sway of the dangling gold triangles at her ears. "I feel as if she's never coming out of there," he said, gesturing with an arm at the turquoise-painted door with the number one and a smiley face on it.

"Easy," she teased.

He noted a gathering of several parents now. They were inching closer to the designated gate where the children would be dismissed.

"Do you mind that I came?"

How could he tell her that time away from her was becoming unbearable. "I'd hoped you would." He squeezed her waist, then motioned with an arm toward the direction she'd come from and the school parking lot. "You didn't drive. How did you get here?"

"Mrs. Sorenson—"

He grinned wryly. "You mean the neighbor to the left? That Mrs. Sorenson?"

"That's the one. She dropped me off."

Aware of movement around them, parents shuffling forward to claim their children, Alex scanned the sea of youthful faces for Shelby's.

"Do you want to stop at home? Maybe Joe learned more."

"He said he wouldn't know anything until tomorrow," Alex answered distractedly.

"There she is." Gillian pointed at Shelby darting her way around classmates to reach them. "And she's smiling."

"Thank God," Alex muttered.

After going home they ate at a restaurant that catered to families, then stopped at an ice-cream parlor for dishes of rocky-road ice cream. A cool evening breeze, light-jacket weather, accompanied their walk from Alex's SUV to the park for the concert. While he helped fan out a red-and-black-plaid blanket near a tree, Shelby talked about her day.

Since leaping into Alex's arms outside the school, she'd been talking. She and Jenna had made friends with two other girls. She'd had so much fun. "Their names are Tyran and Kayla. And my teacher, her name is Mrs. Milton, has a frog in the room, and we have to hang our backpacks on hooks by the door."

Reluctantly she wound down as the musicians tuned their instruments. She loved "The Flight of the Bumblebee," and the beginnings of "Peter and the Wolf," but yawned three times in five minutes.

Gillian doubted she'd last much longer and expected Alex's suggestion that they go home. She noted the smile on his face hadn't left since his daughter started talking.

When they'd settled back in his vehicle, she glanced in her visor mirror, saw that Shelby was asleep in the back seat. Being with them in the quiet darkness, she felt a peacefulness, a sense of rightness she hadn't felt anywhere else. She'd been so certain she hadn't wanted ties. Before she'd arrived, she'd made plans. But she hadn't given much thought to the new job since she'd arrived. She hadn't cared about anything except answers to a family problem and being with Alex and Shelby, helping them whenever she could.

"You're quiet." He reached across the distance between them, caressed her cheek. "Penny for your thoughts."

I like being a part of your life, she wanted to say. "I was thinking that the day went well." She took a long breath. She really wanted nothing permanent. She still had so much to do.

Overnight the air cooled more, and the chill of autumn clung to a northeasterly wind. Her feet pounding against the pavement, Gillian ran at a faster pace than usual this morning. She turned on a road bordered by woods. In the predawn light she stared at the silhouettes of pine trees. Soon she'd trade in the sight of them for palm trees. At Christmastime, while Alex and Shelby played in the snow, she'd be piloting honeymooners between islands.

Dew glistened on grass with the first hint of sunlight. When had she begun to think so much about tomorrows? She used to live her life for the moment.

And if she stayed, what would she do here? Who needed a small-plane pilot? A charter service, she reasoned, one that offered trips over the Grand Canyon or to Las Vegas or Phoenix. She could do anything she wanted here, couldn't she?

But she wasn't staying. She was leaving, going to Hawaii. Plans had been made months ago. Determined to stop thinking so much, in her head she hummed Rod Stewart songs on her way back to the apartment.

"Hello, Gillian." Mrs. Sorenson, Loretta's neighbor, a frail-looking, white-haired woman waved from the front porch of a redbrick bungalow and inched down two steps to get her attention. Gillian stopped. Running in place, she listened and nodded agreeably to the woman's request.

Alex was worrying about her. Every morning, she ran before daybreak. Every morning, he stood at the kitchen window, waiting for her to get back. That she had a brown belt in karate and could probably defend herself better than he could didn't count.

"Are we going to wait for Gillian?" Shelby pushed at a kitchen chair, scraping the legs across the floor.

Alex forced himself to concentrate again on the scrambled eggs in the frying pan. "Probably not." Gillian really wasn't crazy about breakfast.

A memory returned from that field trip nearly five years ago. They'd taken a trip into town for breakfast. While everyone had ordered eggs and pancakes and French toast, she'd gobbled up lemon meringue pie. He'd thought her a nut. He'd been certain she was the last person he would want to spend time with.

Another time, years later, before he'd married, she'd come to visit, showing up unexpectedly at his apartment door with breakfast, a bag of tacos. He'd been so glad to see her that he'd considered eating one. He'd hugged her, and for one brief second had felt the rush of desire. What he'd viewed as good sense then had stopped him, but he felt a twinge of regret now, wishing he'd acted on those feelings.

"Daddy?"

The image of fiery-red hair pulled back in a ponytail, of snug white shorts and long, tanned legs faded. "What do you want, honey?"

"Will you take me to school and pick me up again?"

He pushed the spatula through the mound of yellow in the frying pan. He hadn't planned to. Switching off the burner, he felt torn between a promise to Gillian and his daughter's request. Shelby wouldn't have asked if she hadn't wanted him there.

"Gillian's back," she announced before he could answer. He, too, heard her sneakered footsteps racing up the stairs. As though she'd been gone days instead of an hour, Shelby dashed to her. "Hi, Gillian."

Alex took in her black leotards and an above-the-knee, hot pink sweatshirt before she hunkered down for Shelby's hug. Her hair wilder than usual begged to have fingers buried in it.

"I got a blouse that color, Gillian." Shelby's eyes darted to him. "Daddy, can I wear it today?"

"Go change, but hurry. Breakfast is almost ready." While she rushed out, he ladled spoons of eggs from the frying pan to a plate for Shelby. "I'll make arrangements to have someone take my afternoon classes today and ask Susan, Jenna's mother, to pick up Shelby."

"You don't really want to do that, do you?" Moving close, she frowned at him. "This is only her second day. I'd think you'd want to get her. Anyway—"

"That's some outfit," he murmured close to her ear.

He felt her smiling lips against his cheek. "Thank you."

"Listen," he said more seriously, "you'd be better off going up there in a 4-wheel drive than driving that small compact rental car." He wanted to say,

Don't go without me. He didn't know what she faced, but he didn't want her to be alone.

She offered a careless wave. "We can go tomorrow."

That surprised him. "You're kidding." Was she stalling, suddenly afraid of a confrontation of any kind with Carly Selton? She still possessed the ability to puzzle the hell out of him, Alex realized. "I thought you'd be in a hurry to go."

"Well, I was but we both have things to do."

He always did. His life was full of responsibilities and commitments. He never griped about having too much to do. He believed he'd manage to finish whatever had to be done. If he needed flexibility in his schedule to help her, well then— Then, what? Where had that thought come from? he wondered as she moved away. When did he get so carefree about timetables and daily plans?

"I sort of made a promise yesterday to Mrs. Sorenson when she drove me to the school." She opened a pantry cabinet that was filled with dry goods and cans.

From a distance Alex peered in to see what she was stretching to reach in the back of the cabinet.

"She's supposed to go for dental surgery and will be a little woozy. So she'll need a ride."

Unabashedly he enjoyed the treat before him of her bending over in those tight pants. She straightened, holding a box of the chocolate-flavored, toaster pastries. At the store last week he'd seen them on a shelf, remembered she liked the strawberry-filled ones, and figured this flavor would be a winner for someone who popped chocolates anytime. "Guess you don't want the scrambled eggs."

She dropped two pastries into the toaster slots. "I run to eat *this*, Alex." Turning, she lounged against the counter. "Mrs. Sorenson thought her daughter might be free, but asked me sort of as backup. As it happened, she does need me to drive her. Her daughter has a business meeting."

He loved her kindness, her thoughtfulness. He'd known another woman who'd been full of herself, worrying only about what she felt, what she wanted. Gillian amazed him, always. Because he doubted she'd want the words he was thinking about how sweet and wonderful she was, he did the next best thing. When she started to turn back to the toaster, he snagged her waist and firmly kissed her.

"You're doing it again." Shelby's voice sang. In unison they angled a look to the left. She stood in the doorway, grinning. "You're kissing again."

From Shelby's beaming face, Gillian assumed that met with her approval.

"See my shirt." She pressed her chin to her chest and looked down. "We're the same. Sometimes Jenna and her mommy match."

Mommy. Did Shelby really think of her that way? She'd never considered being a mother until a few days ago. Aware of Shelby's stare, she bent forward and kissed her cheek. "I love the blouse." She didn't say more, couldn't. Shelby's hard hug knotted her throat. With a swift turn away, she snatched up a napkin and the toasted pastries. It might be best to avoid the cozy breakfast scene this morning. "Have a fun day." She tried for normal—casual. Halting beside Alex, she pecked his cheek. "Be good at school," she told him, then rushed toward the door. Behind her, she heard Shelby's giggle over her words to her daddy.

Intentionally she'd gone for a breezy manner. In truth, she needed to leave. Being with them was too easy, too comfortable—too perfect.

Like a child daydreaming about being elsewhere, Alex gazed out the classroom window. Darkening clouds developed in the afternoon sky. Impatience to be home with Gillian and Shelby made him check his watch. Time was dragging.

When she'd taken off this morning, he hadn't realized that he would miss her so much. They were friends. Dammit, no, they were more. Lovers. In love. Only one of them was, he reminded himself.

Annoyed, he gave his students a flash quiz. He ignored their groans. He was miserable without her. Shouldn't everyone feel the same way? But he let them suffer only till the end of the test.

At a minute before the hour, he delivered a parting announcement. "The test results won't count," he said, and left the room ahead of them. At a clipped pace he walked down the hallway, checked his watch again. Unless he ran into a traffic jam, he should reach Shelby on time.

It used to be just the two of them. Would be again. No, they had Joe now. "Let's go to the park," he suggested to his daughter when she was in the vehicle with him.

Pleasure swept over her face. "Can we go on the swings?"

"You bet."

And the way they used to do, he sat on one with her on his lap, his arms wrapped tightly around her. He needed to get used to this again.

At her urging they stopped at the video store, and for the next hour and a half they sat side by side on the sofa and watched a movie about a basketball-playing dog. As the credits rolled on the screen, Shelby's stomach growled. "What was that?" Alex peered at her and teased. "A bear?"

"Daddy!" She laughed, folded when he tickled her belly.

"I'd better make dinner for that bear."

"Can I go downstairs and show Mrs. Yabanski my yellow folder?" The school binder contained her art masterpieces.

"She's not home. She's with Grandpa at the doctor's," he said rather than explain her grandfather had gone for a test.

"They're home. I heard them when you went to the bathroom a little while ago."

Damn. Couldn't Joe come up and tell him the news? "Go ahead. And tell them I'm making dinner tonight," he said, pushing to a stand as she ran ahead of him into the kitchen. Had Joe avoided coming up to tell him because the news was worse than anticipated? Or had Joe thought he wouldn't care? Had they reached that point?

Chapter Eleven

"Hi, Grandpa."

Steps behind Shelby, Alex reached the kitchen doorway to see Joe coming in and closing the outside door. "Loretta made a cake," Joe said, "but wouldn't tell me what kind."

Shelby beamed up at him. "I'll go and ask Mrs. Yabanski what kind of cake."

Joe chuckled at her I'll-take-charge-of-this tone before she hurried out the door, but he looked tired, Alex thought. "What did the test show?" he asked, seeing no point in pretending he wanted to discuss anything else.

His father greeted him with a scowl. "I need to go in for a cataract operation."

Beneath the annoyance in Joe's voice, Alex detected a trace of fear. For such an independent man, this latest illness had to be difficult. The heart attack had been tough on a man used to controlling others. He wished they were closer, that he could go to him, help him. "Don't worry about anything," Alex finally said. If his father rebuffed him, he'd deal with it. "I'll be here for you."

For a second, silence answered him. "What did you say?" he asked in an abrupt tone that used to make Alex cringe as a kid.

"Whatever you have to deal with, we'll do it together."

"Why?"

Tension settled in his gut, knotting it. Had he left himself open to more criticism? Well, too bad if he had. He couldn't let Joe go it alone. "If you need me, I'll be here," he returned sharply.

"You never needed me."

Alex's eyes locked with his father's. "Never needed you?"

"Daddy?" Shelby burst through the back door.

Alex stirred himself from thoughts about the man standing before him, about a sadness in his eyes he'd seen only once before when Alex's mother had died. Was it possible that all these years they'd both wanted the same thing?

Pausing in the doorway behind Shelby, Gillian shoved up the sleeves of the green sweater she'd changed into earlier. "Joe, what did you learn?"

As if still caught up in the previous moment, Joe hesitated before sharing the doctor's words with both of them. "He says only one eye has to be done."

"Oh." Smiling, Gillian rushed to him and hugged him. "That's good news, isn't it?"

"Good...?" When she drew back, Joe returned a weak smile. "Yes, I guess it was good news."

Alex wanted to kiss her right then in front of everyone. She was so good for all of them.

"Daddy, can I help make dinner?"

"Sure you can. Wash your hands and you can make the hamburger patties. Want to do that?"

She flashed a smile at her grandfather. "I like doing that. It feels gushy. Daddy let me do that before."

"Guess I'll set the table," Joe said, seeming in better spirits.

In passing, Gillian touched Alex's hand, gave it an encouraging squeeze, then went toward the door. "And I'm off to the bakery to pick up dessert."

"Wait," Joe called out, but she was out the door. "She doesn't need to go. Loretta made a cake."

It occurred to Alex that she'd known, but had left to give them privacy.

Eager for her task, Shelby skipped in. "My hands are all cleaned."

Though troubled by what Joe had said, Alex concentrated on her instead.

In a few moments Shelby had made two misshapen and uneven hamburger patties. One resembled a meatball. Another one looked like a pancake. "Those look good, Shelby."

For a while the three of them—grandfather, father and daughter—moved around the kitchen like a close-knit unit. And he couldn't stop a thought: he wished Gillian had stayed, been a part of this.

"I'm all done." Shelby grinned wide with satisfaction over her accomplishment.

"Go wash again," he told her, and carefully transferred the odd-shaped patties to a plate. In the back of his mind was the report about midterm curriculum that the dean wanted. It meant several hours of work ahead of him.

"You're good with her. Close," Joe said. "I thought a father's only job was to provide."

Joe's words stilled him.

Was that his father's excuse for never being around for him, for never praising or offering a hug? He supposed they couldn't forget the conversation started before Shelby had come in. Neither of them had ever said so much before about the past. He couldn't place all the blame on Joe's shoulders. As a kid he'd only seen his own side of the situation.

"When I was a child we had nothing," Joe said. "We were what other people called 'dirt poor.'"

Alex knew he'd come from a big family. "Your father owned a farm, didn't he?"

"He was a farmer in Arkansas, but he didn't own any land. He worked it for someone else." He crossed to the sink, made much about filling a glass with water. "There were fourteen of us kids and never enough of anything."

Alex spoke his thought. "You never told me that before."

"Sounds like I'm whining," he replied simply.

"No, it doesn't. It sounds as if times were tough."

His back to him, Joe nodded. "They were." Slowly he turned. As if it took effort, he met Alex's stare. "I never wanted my child to know that kind of life. I wanted more for you."

How often had he complained about Joe being gone, about Joe not giving them a home and stability? But he'd had a lot more than Joe had known. "Was that why you stayed in the military?"

"The life isn't right for everyone. Like you. You wouldn't have liked it. You have a curious mind. You need to be able to question. You always liked learning. I was content to have my basic needs taken care of. And I could never have given you anything if I hadn't stayed in the service. I had no education until I went in. The military gave me everything I wanted for your mother and you. We were able to offer you college. That was a must. You were so smart."

No, he'd been dumb. God, he'd been incredibly dumb. Joe had given him the best he could. "Why didn't you ever tell me that before?"

"In my family, you didn't talk about your feelings or what you didn't have. But—"

Alex didn't move. "What?"

"I'm really proud of what you've done," Joe said suddenly.

Nothing he could have said would have surprised Alex more. His whole life he'd wanted to hear those words from him. "You've never said that before."

"Guess I should have. But I didn't think you needed me to say anything. You were always so sure of yourself. And you had your mother. You were close." He gave an uncharacteristic shrug. "I didn't know how to be a father. You do. You're a good father. A lot better than I was."

"I wouldn't say—"

"Don't!" Joe sliced a hand through the air to silence him. "Take the credit. It's one of the most important jobs in life."

He didn't need anyone to tell him that. He was a teacher. He valued children. "I know."

"I didn't." Joe's voice softened suddenly. "I wish I had known that. Then you might have needed me."

If only he knew how much he'd wanted him in his life. "Needed you?" He gave him a humorless smile. "You're my father." *You're what I needed most.* He yearned to say the words. Maybe someday. Not yet. It would take more than a few moments to mend years of being strangers, but something had happened. For the first time in his life, Alex felt closer to him. "I wish you'd been around more."

Visibly Joe drew a breath. "Did you?"

Standing at the door, Gillian had unintentionally eavesdropped. They'd been too involved in their conversation to even notice her. Backing up, she decided to return to the stairs, then come back. Happiness for Alex filled her. At some moment, in some way, father and son were finding each other. It wouldn't be easy for them.

For her, either. She needed to face the past. What if her father *had* been less than perfect? Did that mean she should forget all the love she'd known from him?

His affair had been before she was born. It was ridiculous to let something that happened in the past destroy wonderful memories. For too long she'd viewed her father unrealistically, expecting him to be some paragon of virtue. But he made mistakes. He wasn't special or perfect—except to her.

"I guess the operation won't be so bad," Joe said while they were eating dinner.

"They might give you ice cream, Grandpa," Shelby piped in. "I got ice cream when they took my tonsils out."

A smile for her erased the grim set of his features. "Maybe they'll give that to me, too. I like strawberry best of all."

Alex looked up with a frown. "Why didn't you say you liked strawberry?" Not once had his father put in a request for it before Alex had gone grocery shopping.

"I eat that other stuff. Like that kind with the chocolate chips."

"And spumoni," Loretta piped in. "Ice cream is your grandpa's weakness," she said conspiratorially to Shelby.

Shelby flashed a smile at him. "Chocolate chip is my favorite, Grandpa."

"Is that right." Gently he patted the top of her head.

Alex figured he'd pack a couple of gallons of strawberry ice cream in the freezer for after his father's operation. "We'll get some strawberry, too." In response to the phone ringing, he shoved back his chair.

While he said hello to the caller, Gillian answered Joe and Loretta's questions about her search.

"Tomorrow might give you answers, then?" Loretta said rather than asked.

"I hope so." Her voice trailed off, curiosity getting the best of her as she saw the look of excitement on Alex's face.

"We need to celebrate." He set down the receiver, rushed to her. Grabbing her at the shoulders, he stood her before him, then gave her a hard, quick kiss.

Looking on, Joe laughed. "Don't do that to me."

"Daddy!" Shelby rose to stand on her chair. "Daddy, why are you...?"

He caught her at the waist. "You're going to have that big bedroom. And you know what else? You're going to have your puppy," he promised as she wrapped her legs around his waist.

While she was yippeeing, he filled Gillian and Joe in on the news. "That was the agent. I'd qualified for a loan long ago. All I had to do was make an offer. I did. The house is ours," he announced.

"Oh, Alex." Gillian gave him an equally hard kiss, now that she knew what they were celebrating. She was happy for all of them. She really was. Really happy. Very happy.

It took work, but Alex quieted Shelby by reading a few books to her at bedtime. Joe left with Loretta for a movie, and Gillian volunteered to wash dishes. Why was she feeling so low suddenly? She'd never been prone to depression. Why now? She set a plate on the drainboard. She had been happy for them, but she'd felt left out, she realized. That had been their celebration, not hers.

She wrestled with a self-pitying mood and stepped outside. Leaning on the back-porch railing, she stared at the silhouette of distant mountains. She felt a chill on her skin, but stayed, letting the cool breeze whip around her. She'd always been so sure what she did and didn't want—until now.

"Aren't you cold?"

As his strong arms came around her, she realized how right this felt and rested her head back on his shoulder. "Not anymore." They stayed like that for moments, quiet, warming each other, then he stepped away. Gillian turned to see him pick up a wineglass from a small table near the doorway. "It went well with Joe this evening."

He handed her a glass then drew her close again. "Better than it's ever been."

"Why don't you look pleased?" she asked. It felt so natural to be with him like this.

"I am." A semblance of a smile was the best he could do. "He never said so much."

That should please him. "Are you in shock?" she asked, because he looked so confused by all that had evolved in one afternoon.

"Somewhat." His gaze met hers, held it. "Thank you for making Joe feel better about the operation. He likes you."

"I'm glad. I like him, too."

"Believe me." Softly he chuckled. "That's a first. He's never liked any female friend of mine except you."

Gillian sipped her wine. Heat from it and him coursed through her. ''Why?''

''Most of them were afraid of him. You aren't?''

She laughed. ''That's me. Fearless. Did he like Nicole?''

''Not at all.'' He raised his face, studied the stars for a moment. There was such hardness in his eyes when he met her stare again.

She knew Nicole had hurt him badly. She assumed there had been another man, but didn't know if he'd existed before they'd decided to divorce or after. She'd never asked. It had been clear to her how painful the failure of his marriage had been to him. And she recalled a time when he'd worried he'd have to fight her for custody of Shelby.

''Shelby looks like her.''

Gillian nodded in agreement. ''Yes, she does. But that's not bad. Nicole was a beautiful woman.''

''Not really. Not in the way that matters.''

She'd heard no bitterness in his voice. Rather he'd spoken in a matter-of-fact tone.

''Months after Nicki left Shelby and me, she called.''

Gillian had thought he'd had no contact with Nicole after she'd left. With only light from the apartment illuminating the porch, his eyes looked like dark slits.

''Do you remember her uncle?''

''Vaguely.'' At Alex's wedding to Nicole, Gillian recalled a gray-haired man with a sour expression and a stiff posture as the one who'd given Nicole away. ''Wasn't he kind of stuffy?

"Definitely. She tried to stay on his good side because of his money. But he wasn't easy to get along with. Pompous, he didn't approve of her lifestyle after she left me, and disowned her. That's why she came to see me. She needed money."

Because he'd never told her that before, Gillian realized how much he'd been hurt by Nicole's actions.

"When I refused, Nicki leveled me with the ultimate threat."

As he stepped away from her, Gillian peered harder at him in the darkness.

"She knew how much I loved Shelby. So she did the obvious. She threatened to take Shelby from me if I didn't give her some money."

She'd never liked Nicole and knew the feeling had been mutual. But Gillian had never thought of her as cruel until that moment. "Alex, she couldn't. You were the parent that took care of Shelby. She walked away, abandoned her child. No court would favor her."

"That's what I thought. I viewed that as an idle threat. After all, I'd been taking care of our daughter."

"Did that stop her?"

"She laughed. They would give Shelby to her, she insisted. I had no rights."

"You're a wonderful father. And the courts do give children to fathers. You had just as much of a chance to—"

"She yelled that I didn't. Shelby wasn't mine."

She caught her breath, astonished. How could anyone be so hurtful?

Pain settled on his face. ''I didn't believe her.''

''Of course, not. She—'' She paused. Why did he look so tormented? ''She was lying.''

''Sure. She was lying. But she rattled on, determined to make me believe her. She went on with details about some old acquaintance she'd run into during a holiday trip when she'd gone to see her uncle in Colorado. I had no choice. I had to be sure. So I took a blood test.''

Gillian's heart stopped as her mind raced ahead of their conversation to words she imagined but as yet hadn't been said.

His eyes returned to hers, and in an instant, his pain reached her. ''It confirmed that she'd been telling the truth. I'm not Shelby's biological father.''

Gillian started to shake her head, searched for some reasoning to make him see that Nicole had lied, but she saw the truth in his eyes.

''It doesn't matter to me. Those are just words,'' he said flatly. ''I've always been her daddy. I always will be.''

''Oh, Alex.'' Her heart ached for him. ''What did you do after learning about this?''

''I paid Nicki.''

''You paid her?''

''I'd do anything for Shelby.'' His fingers tightened on the stem of the wineglass. ''You know that. So I made an appointment with a lawyer to find out what my rights were, because I wasn't ever giving Shelby up.''

She wished he'd shared this with her then. Why hadn't he? "What did he say?"

"Before the appointment with the lawyer, Nicki died in the boating accident, and the problem no longer existed."

Gillian couldn't see how that was possible. There was a father somewhere. But she needed an answer to another question first. "Why didn't you ever tell me about this?"

"You knew about the divorce. You'd only been gone a few days when this all happened. I wasn't going to call you back. Your brother had just passed the bar exam. You went to be with him in Boston to help him get settled."

"Would you have called me if you'd had to go to court?"

"Yes, I would have."

The hurt within vanished instantly. He'd been thinking of her, not wanting to disrupt a good time in her life, she reminded herself. "Why didn't you have to go to court?" she asked, leading up to the next logical question.

In the darkness, she saw his frown. "Why would I? Nicki died."

"What about Shelby's biological father? Where is he?"

"Who knows."

"Alex, you have to be concerned. He could show up one day, demand custody." She'd die inside for him if he had to give up Shelby.

"He won't show. I don't know who he is and doubt I ever will. During Nicki's smug tirade about me not having any rights, she tried to taunt me. Shelby was hers, only hers, she'd insisted. The father didn't know she existed. Who he is is a mystery. All I know is he was married.''

''So there's no one else?'' How could only Alex treasure that beautiful little girl? There was another blood relative, Gillian remembered. ''Nicole's uncle.''

Alex pulled a face. ''Uncle Hubert? I don't think so. With his puritanical attitude, he'd never accept Shelby. In his eyes she's the child of an illicit affair.''

''Does anyone else know this?'' Gillian asked.

''No one but you.''

Having seen how devoted they were to each other, Gillian doubted he regretted the decision to keep Shelby, to make her his own forever despite what Nicole had told him.

He confirmed her thought. ''Shelby is mine now. Will always be. I made a mistake marrying Nicki, but I don't regret a day of that time with her. Without her, I wouldn't have had Shelby.''

''She's so lucky to have you.'' Gillian bridged the distance between them and slipped an arm around his back. ''So am I.''

Laughter colored his voice. ''Is that so?''

''Yes, that's so. Where's Joe?'' she asked when he placed a hand beneath the hem of her sweater, caressed the skin at her waist.

''He's staying at Loretta's until moving day. But according to him neither of them is ready to make the arrangement permanent yet.''

"And Shelby's sleeping?" She ran her fingers along the short stubble of his beard.

She laughed as he backed her into the apartment. "Shelby's sleeping."

When they reached the living room doorway, he hit the lightswitch. Beneath the mantle of darkness, she watched his eyes turn darker, then his head lowered and his lips closed over hers. She swayed closer, tasted the drugging sweetness of him when his tongue sought hers. His hands moved through her hair, down to her shoulders, gently stroked her arms. The fire simmered just beneath the surface. With the taste of him filling her mouth, an urgency swept through her. Her arms tight on his back, she staggered a few more steps. "Here," she begged and sank to the rug, drawing him down with her.

Hands tugged at cloth. He pulled up her sweater; she sought the zipper on his jeans. Kisses grew hungrier. Hearts thudded harder. She could barely see his face, but felt harsh breaths on her face while he undressed her.

Just as his mouth seduced, his touch enticed. How had she gone all these years without him? He ran a hand lightly down her ribs, stroked the back of her knee, nibbled her hip, kissed her breast. On a breath she whispered his name as his mouth skimmed her thigh. Then the magic of his tongue torched a fire within her. She writhed beneath each caress, each tantalizing stroke, cried out his name as his tongue plunged into her. Pleasure burst through her. Stunned, she lost a sense of time while she waited for her breathing to even out. For seconds, she'd known nothing, she'd been beyond reason.

Now, she shifted, glided her tongue across his chest, down his stomach. She tasted and touched. She craved the saltiness of his flesh.

Through a cloud of sensation, she heard his raspy murmur. Her name on his lips, he rose above her to reach for the condom in his wallet.

For a moment she stared at his bent head. Then he raised his beautiful face, damp and tense with need. Eyes dark with passion met hers before his lips captured hers again. With a soft moan she snaked arms and legs around him. Her thoughts were only of him. Feel him. Fill herself with him.

Huskily he murmured something against her throat. She wished for words to tell him what he made her feel. She couldn't talk. Even breathing was an effort as he moved within her, ground against her. She gripped him tighter. Bodies pounded to keep pace with the passion sweeping over them. All that might never be said between them resounded through the room on each whisper, each moan. And mindless to everything, she journeyed with him to the one place she wanted to stay.

Chapter Twelve

Gillian had planned to be gone from his bed before morning. But after he'd carried her to his room, she'd fallen asleep in his arms. Rays of sunlight bathed the bedroom with a warm glow, and, too comfortable to move, she cuddled closer. "I feel wonderful."

Slowly his fingers skimmed her spine and settled on the curve of her backside. He spoke words to suit him. "Yes, you do. But my back feels as if someone walked on it. Why didn't we go to bed like sensible people?"

Her laughter drifted over him. "We were being spontaneous."

Featherlight his fingers floated up again, then followed her ribs to rest on her hipbone. "Could we be spontaneous in bed from now on?"

"Anywhere you want."

His grin came quickly. "In the bed."

"I should get up." Halfheartedly, she spoke the words, unable to move as he rained kisses down to her breast.

"It's early. Shelby won't be up yet."

With fingertips she grazed his hip, the hard plane of his thigh. "You might be late if—"

"It's okay."

"Okay?" She couldn't help laughing. "It's okay if you're late?" Her voice trailed off when he lowered his head. "Alex—"

"Don't leave yet," he murmured.

She sucked in breath. "Not yet."

She left him just barely before Shelby awakened. Another two minutes by his side and they'd have been drilled with questions by a five-year-old.

Dressed in pajamas, a yawning Shelby shuffled into the kitchen. "What are you making? Pancakes?"

Now there was a challenge. *Oh, why not?* Gillian mused. "Okay?"

While Shelby padded out to head for the bathroom, Gillian mixed the batter. She had several pancakes in the skillet when she called Mildred Nevins with a question. She managed a second call, too, before Shelby returned with Alex trailing her.

"They look good," he said, craning his neck to see in the skillet.

"Real good," Shelby said.

Gillian placed a hand on her slim shoulder.

"Thank you." She would miss this. The closeness that she'd found with Alex, what she'd found with Shelby. Children had been Rachel's dream. But Gillian, since being around Shelby, understood why her sister viewed a child as one of life's treasures.

"Something smells good," Joe said, ambling in from the back door.

"Blueberry pancakes." To her satisfaction, they looked pretty good. And the small kitchen, brimming with people, seemed cozy rather than uncomfortable.

Joe looked in a lot better frame of mind this morning. The night with Loretta had obviously worked wonders. Midway through their meal he told Alex, "You and Gillian can leave whenever you're ready."

"I have one class first."

"Go when you're ready. I'll take Shelby to school today."

Shelby's face lit. "You will, Grandpa?"

A warmth was in the room, Gillian thought. With Joe's offer, it seemed that he was making an effort to work with Alex, to make them a family.

Plopping down on a chair, Shelby picked up her fork. "That's good 'cause you can come in and see my teacher's frog."

"Horace," Joe informed Alex and Gillian while he joined his granddaughter at the table.

A sparkle of amusement lingered in Alex's eyes. Gillian felt herself, smiling, too. It was so nice to see him enjoying his father.

"Okay, you two go to school, see the frog." In passing, Alex let his fingers brush her hip. "We can leave as soon as I'm back from class.'' He turned away in response to the phone. ''I'll—''

Closest to it, Gillian snatched up the receiver. ''Got it.''

Though staying meant being late, Alex glued his feet to the floor, stalling, nursing the last swallow of the breakfast drink when he heard her say the caller's name.

''Reed, it's good to hear from you.''

Alex wanted to hear more, but her back turned on them, and while she talked, the room flowed with movement. Shelby hugged Gillian, and him, then trailed her grandfather out the door to stay with Loretta and him until schooltime. Still waiting, he watched the door close behind his father and daughter.

Facing him, Gillian set down the telephone. ''That was Reed.'' As if he didn't know. ''He said his extra plane should be there by Thursday.''

Alex made a guess at what else was said. ''He wants you to come now?''

''I wasn't sure if I'd be done here by then.'' At the sink she plucked a fork from the bottom of the dishwater. ''We hadn't felt there was a big rush for me to get there before this. He only had two planes. Until he got his third, I had nothing to fly.''

''What did you tell him?''

Head down, she dried her hands on a dish towel. ''I told him that something personal is happening. In a few days, I might have more answers.''

What could he say? *Don't go.* He couldn't ask her not to leave. Bridging the space between them, he kissed her hard, wanted to imprint his mark on her. He wanted more than this moment, but he would never ask her to stay. Never. "I'll be back soon," he promised, then stepped out of the apartment.

Dull. Your life is dull. I hate it, Nicki had screamed at him. He couldn't stand to see the same look in Gillian's eyes.

Gillian waited for her breathing to calm. Had she imagined a desperation in his kiss? *I'm going to miss you,* she'd wanted to say. He excited her more than any man ever had. He ignited a fire within her, one that had kindled as if waiting for him. She hadn't known she could feel like that, but she had to be realistic. This was never meant to be more than an affair.

They were too different. Sometimes she was amazed that they were such good friends. They shouldn't have been. She liked Thai food and rhythm and blues. He liked meat loaf and classical music. He found comfort in a good book. She relaxed by scuba diving.

She had to get a grip. Why was she thinking so much about the two of them? She should be planning to leave. She should have given Reed a firm answer about when she'd come. But she had a good reason for not doing that. She needed to get answers about Carly first.

What would Rachel and Sean want her to do? Days ago when she'd informed them that Carly was alive, all of them had been in such shock that they hadn't made solid plans about what Gillian should do when she made contact.

"I'm going to welcome her into our lives," she said minutes later when talking to her brother. She cradled the phone between her jaw and shoulder and dried her hands on a paper towel. "Is that all right with you?"

"We all knew this would have been the plan if she'd been alive."

"Do you think Rachel will want to?" Gillian asked.

Her brother laughed softly. "She of the generous heart?"

Some tension oozed out of her. "I'll call Rachel, then, before I leave."

"Good luck."

"Thanks." Less uncertain, she punched out Rachel's phone number. As expected, her older sister agreed immediately.

With a plan set in her mind, she made one more call before rushing into the shower. She dressed for the trip in black jeans and a rust-colored, V-neck top, and fifteen minutes later, while she was pouring freshly made coffee into a thermos, the back door opened. She expected to see Joe, not Alex. He couldn't be done with his class yet. "You're back already?"

"I figured you've waited long enough to get your answers. I called another teacher to take my morning class."

"I might not even see Carly today," she said, more nervous than she'd expected. When he came near, she automatically stepped into his calming embrace. The conditions she'd placed on other relationships didn't work with him. He stretched every emotion, forced her to feel more. And he gave more than any man she'd ever known. "Isn't this insane? This is what I wanted. And now," she admitted, trying to laugh at herself, "now I'm learning I have a yellow streak down my back."

Faint smile lines fanned out from the corners of his eyes. "I hadn't noticed."

Gillian tipped up her chin. "You just don't see it."

Softly he pressed a kiss to her nose. "Trust me. I didn't see one."

His tease steadied her. "You didn't?"

"Nope. And I looked you over really well." Pleasure sparked in his eyes. "Really well."

The hours on the road failed to settle her nerves, Alex guessed. He observed her frown and wished for a way to ease her mind. This couldn't be easy. When she came face-to-face with Carly, would she change her mind about welcoming a stranger into her family?

While she viewed the woods, he drove slowly over a rutted road. Edith had chosen to live out in no-man's-land on the rim of the White Mountains. Two miles separated her cabin and her closest neighbor's.

He rolled down the window, let the coolness of mountain air drift into the vehicle. From a nearby tree a crow cawed. On the right side of the dirt road a squirrel scurried up a birch with a pine cone. As the breeze ruffled Gillian's hair, temptation slithered through him to caress the soft strands the way he had last night. He wished he could halt time, hold her close.

"I think it's that one," she said with a nervous edge to her voice. Head bent, she skimmed a finger along the hand-drawn map Mildred had given them to Edith's house, then pointed again at an A-frame.

"No one knows you're coming. You can change your mind," he reminded her even as he braked at the side of the road.

"Edith knows. I contacted Mildred for Edith's phone number and called her this morning while you were at the university. I asked her if she'd mind talking to me."

Alex switched off the ignition. Only one reason for doing that made sense to him. After getting the woman's approval to come, ingrained politeness would prevent her from backing away and not going. "What did she say to you?"

"I thought she'd pretend she didn't understand what I was talking about, but she didn't, Alex. She simply asked me what time I was coming. She sounded sad, and—as if she'd been expecting me to come one day. I don't understand that."

Shifting, he draped an arm over the steering wheel. "She did know about her sister's affair with your dad, and about Carly."

"Yes, she's been part of the deception." She drew a long breath. "That's one of the things that bothers me the most. Why were Rachel, Sean and I deceived?''

He sensed that unless she uncovered a good reason for the deception, she'd never accept what her father, Lenore, and Edith had done. ''Yes or no?'' he asked. ''Are we going in?''

Before answering, she gripped the door handle. ''I didn't come this far to turn back.'' While he rounded the front of the Bronco, she slid out. ''Potted red geraniums,'' she said absently.

''What did you say?'' he asked and wished for the impossible at this moment...the sight of her smile.

She motioned toward the pot of flowers outside the front window. ''My mother loved red geraniums, too,'' she said as an explanation.

Other than roses and daisies, he didn't know the name of flowers. He placed a hand on her back while they strode up the walkway, felt her draw more than one deep, calming breath. There were no words to make this moment easier. He didn't doubt she felt conflict, wanting to get answers and afraid of them. Aware of her tension, he swore under his breath that it took so long for someone to answer her knock on the door.

When the door opened, he stared into the eyes of a petite woman. In her early sixties, her gray hair cut in a boyish style, she slowly inched back from the door. ''Come in.'' Adjusting the pale-blue shawl draped around her shoulders, she led the way across a wood plank floor to a small sitting room with a floor-to-ceiling window and a view of the woods at the back of the cabin.

Alex sat beside Gillian on a moss-green sofa across from the woman. Even though she was aged and sickly, her beauty lingered. He appreciated it, but frowned when briefly the woman's eyes met his. What was it about them? What bothered him about her looks? To stop an urge to stare at her, he scanned the room.

"I've been ill," she said, indicating that she'd noticed his interest in the prescription bottles lined up on the end table near her flowered, upholstered chair.

"I'm sorry to bother you," Gillian said, "but this is important to me."

"You look so much—" Edith Selton quieted abruptly in the manner of someone who wished for her words back. "You're so lovely."

"Thank you." Gillian smiled wanly beneath Edith's lengthy study. "Ma'am, you know—"

Lines in the woman's face deepened. "I know about all of it. It's the biggest burden I've ever carried," she said softly. "Let me assure you, my sister never meant to harm anyone."

Before entering the house, Gillian had decided she couldn't handle this woman with kid gloves and get answers. "Your sister deceived my father," she said bluntly. "She led him to believe the child she carried was dead."

Edith fingered the fringe at the end of the shawl. "You must understand. She wanted children. She was a good mother."

Gillian wanted to scream at the woman. She wasn't interested in hearing Edith's praise for her sister. If all she knew was true, then Lenore Selton had nearly destroyed her parents' marriage, had broken her parents' hearts when she'd backed out of the agreement to let them have the child. "I don't understand any of this. When we talked to your friend Mildred, she gave us the impression that Carly was living in town. Is she nearby? I want to meet her. Will you call her?"

Her heart was too big, too generous, Alex decided. He was surprised she didn't get hurt more often. She was so caring that she was ready to reach out with welcoming arms to a woman she didn't even know.

"She—" Edith looked up, past Gillian to the doorway. "My niece is here."

With a look over his shoulder, Alex knew then what bothered him about Edith.

Slowly Gillian rose to face the woman she'd been looking for. Would her sister look like her? Would she have the same hair color as Rachel or Sean or herself? An instant later her legs went weak. Her breath caught in her throat. A woman who looked like her stood by the door. A woman who looked identical to her.

"Carly, this is Gillian."

"What is this?" The woman staring hard at her had paled. "Aunt Edith!" Her voice rose with an accusation. "I don't understand. How could this be?"

"This is your twin, Carly."

Gillian rocked back. Legs promised to buckle. Her world was shifting. "Who...?" She cast a hard look at Edith Selton. Oh, God, this wasn't possible. This couldn't be possible. *My mother's name is Mary Ann, not Lenore. Please, this can't be real.* She wanted to wake up. She wanted this to be just some convoluted dream. The woman she'd thought of as her mother all her life hadn't been the one who'd given birth to her. The siblings she'd grown up with were her stepsister and stepbrother.

Her whole life had been a lie.

"I'm so sorry about all of this." Edith shrank before their eyes, her thin shoulders pulling in. "Carly, I'm sorry. I'm really sorry."

"Aunt Edith?" Carly stepped further into the room. "Explain this. Please," she pleaded. "I don't understand. Who...?" Her hand, palm up, motioned at Gillian.

Gillian looked at Alex, sank back to the cushion beside him and gripped his hand. It was too much to grasp.

"Is she really...?" Carly stopped as if the words hurt.

"Your mother begged me, swore me to secrecy. I knew it was wrong. But too many years had gone by when your mother died," Edith said as an explanation. "Even though I knew you deserved to know the truth, I couldn't bring myself to admit to you what I'd done. You believed in me. After your mother died, you were like the child I never had. I didn't want to lose you, so I didn't tell you."

"Tell me now," Carly insisted, reaching back like a blind person and groping for the cushion of the settee because she couldn't take her eyes off Gillian.

Like Carly, Gillian, too, searched the face of her sister, studied the eyes, the nose, the mouth for differences. There were none except for their hairstyles. Unlike Gillian's long, curly hair, Carly wore hers chin length, straight with bangs. They could have been looking in a mirror.

"I was selfish. I cheated you of a family, Carly." Edith's green eyes had paled, turned watery.

Gillian saw a resemblance to this woman now. The eyes were like her own. Numb, she felt as if she was watching a two-character play. She didn't move, could barely breath.

"Your mother had an affair with Alan Quinn when his wife was ill."

Pain visibly appeared on Carly's face. "My God. How could she?"

"Oh, no, don't misunderstand," Edith appealed. "It was a mental illness. Alan was lost, grieving, aching. At first Lenore said that she felt so bad for him. She reached out as a friend might. She wanted to comfort him. But she grew to love him. She couldn't stop herself. She'd begun to see him often. Possibly he was looking for only a friend, someone to listen to him for his wife had been institutionalized by then. And then one night—"

"Why was his wife in a hospital?" Carly demanded.

"It was only one night?" Gillian cut in.

"Yes. Lenore said that your father felt so guilty."

As Edith dabbed a tissue at her eyes, Gillian took over, offering her side of the story. She told Carly about the baby her mother had lost, and had mourned inconsolably that her father had been alone.

"According to my mother—" Gillian drew another hard breath. *She's not your mother.* "According to her diary, she planned to adopt Lenore's baby, but Lenore had changed her mind and planned to keep the baby. Another journal disclosed that Lenore told them the baby had died."

Quiet, Carly had stared at her as if waiting for Gillian to say something that would make sense. Disbelief now colored her voice. "She told them the baby died? Meaning me?"

Edith cleared her throat. "Lenore was unhappy," she offered as an explanation instead of answering her. "She'd fallen in love with your father."

"Who was he?" Carly questioned. "Who was Alan Quinn?"

Gillian considered all the questions in Carly's mind. She knew many more answers than this woman did. How confused she must be.

The silence made Alex take over. "Alan Quinn was a history teacher. He worked at the same school as Lenore in Maine."

"Maine." Carly repeated as if digesting information. "And my mother thought he'd leave his wife for her?"

Gillian straightened her back at Carly's question.

Edith answered the hard question. "He was honest with Lenore. He loved his wife and children."

"Children?" Gillian hadn't thought it possible for more color to drain from Carly's face until that moment.

"There are three of us," Gillian said to Carly's unspoken question. "Rachel is the oldest. Sean is—"

"Younger or older than us?"

Us! Gillian's heart twisted. "He's older, and a lawyer in Boston. Rachel lives in Maine where her husband owns charter tour boats." *I'm sorry,* she wanted to say. The woman's eyes, so much like her own, carried such torment.

"Lenore fantasized, wanted to believe he would choose her over his wife," Edith said.

Gillian gathered an impression of an honorable woman before her, one who'd struggled to keep a secret for decades. But though Edith might have found her younger sister's actions difficult to overlook, she'd gone along with them. Out of loyalty? Gillian wondered. She knew about that kind of loyalty. She'd do anything for Rachel and Sean, for Alex. "Did Lenore lie to my parents out of spite?"

"Oh, no." With a look, Edith appealed first to Gillian, then to Carly. "Don't misunderstand. Believe me. She wouldn't do that."

There was a time when Gillian might have accepted such words, but all the deceptions made her wonder if she could believe what anyone was saying. She was silent, gathering strength. "But she did lie about the baby, didn't she?'' she asked, unable to keep the challenge out of her voice.

"Yes, she did. But she felt awful doing that, lying to Alan Quinn. She always said he was the only man she'd ever loved.''

"Then why did she lie?'' Gillian blocked her anger as quickly as it formed. Edith is sick, she reminded herself. "I'm sorry. I'm—''

Edith raised a frail-looking, speckled hand. Understanding crept into her eyes. "You have every right to be angry. Both of you do." She clenched her hands and stared at them. "Lenore burst into tears after the phone call to him. She told me how much your father loved children, that she knew this would devastate him.''

That was the man Gillian knew.

"But Lenore wanted to keep the baby." She squeezed her eyes for a second. "You have no idea how much.''

Carly forced the moment. "She only kept one. Why did she keep one twin and give the other away?''

Gillian pressed fingers to her forehead and rubbed the pounding above her eyes. *Why didn't she want me?* "My father knew about two babies?'' she asked, preventing Edith from responding. All her life she'd felt loved. She wasn't sure she wanted to know the answer to Carly's question.

"Not before you two were born." Edith responded so softly that Gillian hunched forward to hear her. "He didn't know until after.''

Gillian swallowed hard. Her throat felt raw. "And then he thought one child had died," she said in his defense as she began to weave her way through the web of deceit. Her gaze shifted to Carly. "But she hadn't."

"Aunt Edith, is all of this true? Is that what happened?"

"Yes. Lenore kept you and contacted him about taking the other baby." She stared at Gillian. "You."

"Why? Why would she do this?" Carly asked.

Gillian wasn't sure she wanted to hear the answer.

Chapter Thirteen

"**Y**ou were much smaller than Carly," she said to Gillian, "and would require a lot more attention and doctoring. My sister honestly didn't think she could handle the medical bills."

Carly swung an inquisitive stare at Gillian. "Is that true? Were you ill?"

Gillian nodded. *How strange it was to stare at yourself. She has my hair. I have her hair.* "I had heart problems. Is that why Lenore got rid of me?" she asked Edith. She couldn't keep the bitterness out of her voice. Shock led her. Who wouldn't feel that way? She'd just been told that her own mother hadn't wanted her. The only reason for Lenore's actions seemed to be her illness.

"Lenore would have kept both of you if she could have handled the bills. But you were quite ill."

Gillian knew that was true. She'd required nearly a decade of doctoring and hospital stays because of heart trouble. "But why did she say the one had died?"

"She was afraid. At first, she changed her mind, refused to give up her baby, but after she had twins, and learned about your illness, she knew she had to let go of you. That's when she contacted Alan again, that's when she told him there had been twins. She was afraid Alan and his wife wouldn't be satisfied to have only the one girl, that they'd want both girls. So she told them that one had died. She said she was willing to let him have the surviving child. He believed her. There was no reason not to, especially after she explained that you were ill."

Quiet through the past few moments, Alex squeezed Gillian's hand to get her attention. "Wasn't there any clue in your mother's diary that twins existed?"

Gillian thought hard about what Rachel had told her about the diary. "Nowhere did she mention twins. Rachel had read in the diary that Lenore had changed her mind. We assumed there had been only one baby." Gillian knew she had to come to terms with this. But she wasn't ready. She didn't know when she would ever be ready.

Edith spoke hesitatingly. "There wouldn't have been. Lenore hadn't known herself about the twins until after she'd called and told him she planned to keep her baby. Then, before the birth, the doctor heard one strong heartbeat because of the way the babies were positioned."

Gillian's eyes strayed to Carly. Her heart opened for her. So far she'd been thinking only about herself. But this woman had to have endured similar pain. How long had she believed her father wanted no part of her? Gillian released Alex's hand. She and Carly had been apart too long. At one time, in the womb, they'd been as one.

Though uncertain about what to do, she nudged herself up from the sofa. Her eyes met and stayed on Carly's as she crossed to her. "Carly, we need—" She sat beside her on the sofa, faced her. As if no other words were needed, Carly nodded. They'd been apart since birth, but in that instant Gillian sensed they were bound by something unexplainable. A private language, a silent one seemed to exist. Was this the unique way of a twin? she wondered. Did they share a special kind of bonding?

"I'm sorry," Carly said then.

No one could understand what she felt except this woman, Gillian knew in that moment and reached for her hands. "I'm sorry, too." She met the eyes so like her own. "Your whole life you must have wondered about Dad. He was wonderful," Gillian told her. "I wish you'd known him. But there are people you need to meet. You have another sister and a brother."

Carly's lips curved in a weak smile. "A stepsister and brother, you mean."

Gillian sensed her hesitation. "Trust me. They're my sister and brother. They'll take one look at you and be yours, too, now."

"I...always wanted a family. I always wished for a brother or sister."

"Now you have a bunch of us."

Edith's shoulders drooped. She looked broken. "Can you both ever forgive me? I did what my sister asked." Her eyes swam with tears. "But I can see now how wrong, how terribly wrong this was."

Gillian didn't know the woman. Though angry about the deception, she couldn't target anyone to blame. Lenore—her mother, was gone. She'd made the choices. Out of love, it seemed. How could she be angry at someone who was dead, someone she didn't know?

Carly, however, had a lifetime of knowing her mother had kept a secret from her. Yet there was no resentment in her voice. "It's all right, Aunt Edith. None of this is your fault."

Gillian wasn't sure she believed her forgiving words. Possibly Carly had said that for obvious reasons. Edith was ill, perhaps dying. But clearly Carly possessed a kind heart. She was like their father. Open and caring. And in that moment, when this stranger with her face went to the older woman and wrapped her arms around her, Gillian stopped worrying if she, Rachel and Sean would like her. She knew they would.

She and Alex stayed longer than Gillian ever intended, but she was reluctant to leave. Carly stared at wallet-size photos Gillian had of her mother and father, and of Rachel and Sean.

''I wish—'' Carly paused, blinked hard for a second.

Gillian understood the words not said. She'd looked at photos of Lenore and had seen the resemblance, and just as Carly wished she'd met their father, Gillian, too, knew she'd always wonder about her real mother, what she'd been like, how her voice had sounded.

With nightfall she rose to leave. Joe and Loretta had been taking care of Shelby since this morning. Though they probably had gone to bed by now, Alex wouldn't feel at ease until he was home with his daughter.

After a promise to Carly to call the next day and make plans for Sean and Rachel to meet her, she stepped outside with Alex.

''Talk to me,'' he urged, slipping an arm around her waist.

''I'm...a mess,'' she said on a laugh that carried no humor. ''I'm happy to find her. And I feel so sad. Does this make any sense?''

''What else?''

''Oh, Alex, it hurts so much. I can't believe this.'' At the pressuring touch of his fingers, she came to a halt and let him embrace her. ''I stared at her and still didn't believe this. All these years, how could I have a sister, no, a twin, and not have felt something?'' The ache squeezed in her chest. A wave of what she interpreted as grief descended on her for the mother who'd raised her. ''The woman I loved isn't my mother.''

''Gillian.'' Tilting her face toward his, he kissed

her lightly. "Don't do this to yourself. Think. Just because a woman is your biological mother, that doesn't mean she'll give you the most love."

"The mother I knew gave it to me, but—she's not my mother."

He forced her eyes to meet his. "Of course she is. You know about Nicki. She was never a real mother to Shelby. Does it matter who gave you birth?"

She knew those weren't just words to offer her solace. He truly believed what he was saying.

She slid her hands from his waist to his back. He was so right. Love for a child made someone the real parent. He loved Shelby more than Nicki ever could have. And the mother she'd always loved had understood that or she wouldn't have agreed to adopt her, to take another woman's child.

She was more than grateful for his comforting words and for the quietness he gave her during the drive home to think about everything. She doubted there was any person in the world who knew her so well, who knew what she needed as much as he did.

Not until he negotiated the final turn toward the house did he break the silence. "You should call your brother and sister."

"Oh, God, Alex." She fought the knot in her throat. "This won't be easy."

He switched off the ignition and shifted toward her. "You talked a good game to Carly about how Sean and Rachel would accept her. Don't you believe what you said?"

"Yes. Yes, I do, but—"

His eyes prodded her to tell him more. ''There's no way I'm going to let you stop there.''

''It's a dumb thought.'' She shrugged a shoulder, actually felt silly saying her thought aloud, but it was one she couldn't rid herself of.

''You can share dumb thoughts with me.''

A laugh bubbled up. It was the last thing she'd expected to do this afternoon. ''You're so good for me.''

''Funny.'' He leaned forward, kissed her brow. ''I always thought that about you. Now what's your dumb thought?''

''You won't laugh, will you?''

For emphasis he crossed his heart. ''Promise.''

''I was thinking the blood between me and Sean and Rachel is watered down.''

He didn't laugh. Sadness clouded his eyes. ''That's not like you. Do you really believe that?''

Emotion, too much to deal with, knotted her throat. Tears smarted her eyes, promising to flow. Feeling fragile, breakable, she wished for the cushion of his arms. ''What if Rachel and Sean do?''

''Gillian.'' Without another word, he pulled her against him.

What would she have done without him? Her arms on his back, she held him tightly to her. She'd needed him more than he could imagine, more than she'd ever expected.

''Don't do that to yourself,'' he said against her hair. ''They love you. A lifetime of love can't be wiped away so easily.'' With a finger he touched her chin, lifted her face to him. "I went through all these years believing no love existed with Joe."

"And it always has," she finished for him. He was so strong, so steady. He made her feel so secure. And though he represented everything she thought she didn't want, at this moment he was everything she needed.

"It always will be there," he said quietly. "That's what you have with Rachel and Sean. And now with Carly. You're all family. You always will be," he reminded her.

At the apartment she held on to those words like a lifeline and punched out her sister's phone number. Edgy, she paced the room while she waited for Rachel's hello.

"Shelby's with Joe down at Loretta's," Alex said from the doorway. "He left a note." In passing, he curled a hand at the back of her neck and kissed her cheek, then left to give her privacy.

His tenderness almost undid her. Alone, she struggled not to fall apart, break down. But her voice broke when she told Rachel all she'd learned. The moment she said that Carly was her twin, it was deadly quiet. Rachel's disbelief and questions followed, then sympathy.

"This was what you were afraid of when you first read about a baby in the diary, isn't it?" Gillian asked.

"Yes, I worried. I didn't know how to tell you that you might be adopted." There were tears in her voice, and Gillian felt all the love her big sister had given her all her life. Rachel drew a deep breath, waited. "Give me a sec." She took another breath. "I feel so badly for you. This must be so hard."

"Rachel, I'll be fine. I'm shocked, but—"

"Honey, I'll catch the first plane out of here. You need us."

"I only need to know that you would come," Gillian assured her. "I love you."

"And I love you."

Sean said the same thing. He exhibited anger, sounding as if he wanted to hit something. Clearly all his emotion was for her. Alex had helped her realize that nothing was different unless she wanted it to be. This was her brother, the one who'd defended her against a neighborhood bully, who'd spent hours at night helping her with algebra, who'd been her hero. He still was. Nothing had changed. "Will you be off and running again after we meet Carly?" Sean asked when he'd finally finished questioning her about Carly.

"I'm not running from anything," she insisted, and laughed at his odd comment. Why had he said that? Her leaving wasn't about running from anything. She chose to be free. She'd led an uncomplicated life by choice. She'd avoided a commitment of the heart. She stayed on the move because she liked change. "There's no reason to stay here, though. I have a job waiting for me in Hawaii." If she was wondering about the other side of life where she'd know from day to day exactly what she'd be doing and with whom, that was natural. But that kind of life wasn't for her.

"You will be there until after we come this week-end?" he questioned.

"Of course, I'll stay until after this weekend." Hearing a sound behind her, she angled a look back. Alex stood in the kitchen doorway for only a second. *Sorry,* he mouthed about intruding, then disappeared.

"You take care, little sister. I love you. See you this weekend," Sean assured her.

Gillian said goodbye, waited a second to gather her composure, then joined Alex in the living room.

"Not as bad as you expected?" he asked, looking up from the magazine in his hands.

"They're wonderful."

Not waiting for her to close the space between them, he pushed to a stand. "You knew that before you called them, didn't you?" he asked, meeting her halfway.

"Yes." For another night she wanted to be with him. "So are you."

Slowly he smiled. "I was going to say that." Idly he caressed the back of her neck. "Come with me."

For a little longer she'd go anywhere with him. She leaned into him to feel his heat. For a little longer there was time for them. "Want something?" she whispered in the shadowed room as he slipped his hands beneath her knit top.

"You," he murmured before his mouth took hers in greedy kiss.

There's no reason to stay here. Two days had passed since Alex had heard her words, and they still hurt a lot more than he'd expected.

All his life he'd analyzed everything. Now all he could do was feel. He didn't need to dissect the emotion inside him that existed for her. He loved her. When it had happened remained a mystery to him. Maybe close to half a decade ago he'd fallen in love with her and had been too dumb to recognize how deeply he felt for her. But he did now. And there was nothing he could do to change what was going to happen.

Looking up, he dodged several students engaged in conversation and saw Gillian dressed in a black sweater and jeans waiting beside his car. At breakfast this morning Joe had volunteered to drop her off so she could meet him for their trek to the grocery store to get cardboard boxes.

Yesterday he'd hauled packing boxes home, and in between working on lectures, grading papers, playing mom, and chauffeuring, he'd packed. The big weekend was coming up. For them and for Gillian. She'd have a family meeting before leaving for Hawaii. He, Joe and Shelby would move into a new home.

He hated packing, always had. He'd more than done his share of it for years. If he had his way, this would be his last move. This house would be the one he would raise his daughter in, grow old in. That was what he wanted, but would he be alone in it? Would there ever be a child's laughter other than Shelby's?

Again he stared at Gillian, responded to her wave to let her know he'd seen her. An unspoken agreement existed. When she left, all they'd shared would end.

"Alex," a masculine voice called out, breaking through his thoughts.

Stopping for Grant, he noticed, from the corner of his eye, Gillian hoisting herself to the hood of his Bronco and swinging denim-clad legs and sneakered feet. "If this is about another blind date candidate, Grant—"

His friend chuckled. "Hardly." His mustache twitched up with his smile at Gillian. "Didn't you notice that everyone backed off? Who is seeing whom fascinates everyone. You know that."

He spoke truth. Within the university community, gossip traveled with the swiftness of a comet.

"They've assumed you found your own love interest." Pointedly his gaze swept toward Gillian, and he waved.

"Why? Because she's living with me?"

"Because it's obvious to everyone that you're in love with her. The first time I met her I thought she seemed so right for you."

Alex wanted to believe that, throw caution to the wind and tell her what he felt and see what happened. But that wasn't his way.

"You two get along so well."

"We don't. We—" What was he going to say? They did get along. They had fun. They were attuned to the other's needs and moods. They were best friends. Damn, why was this suddenly so difficult? He yearned to beg her to stay.

"I'm right, aren't I?" Grant flashed a smug grin and cupped a hand over Alex's shoulder. "Teasing you wasn't my purpose. I came to invite you to dinner next Monday on Deanna's day off from work. You and Gillian.''

She won't be with me. He couldn't get the words out. ''Is there a special reason...?''

''I have to tell you now or I might burst.''

From a distance Gillian watched the two men share what appeared to be wonderful news as Alex hugged his friend. He was still smiling when he left Grant and approached her. ''Something is going on,'' she said more than asked.

Sidling close, he placed his hands at her waist to ease her feet to the ground. He would have liked to feel her body slither along his, but it wouldn't do for Professor Alex Hunter to make out with a gorgeous redhead in the parking lot. ''Grant told me good news. Deanna is pregnant.''

''Oh, Alex.'' A smile shot across her face. ''How wonderful.''

''It is. They'll be great parents.''

''He looked excited.''

His hand linked with hers. ''He invited me to his house for dinner Monday. To celebrate with them. They're inviting a few close friends. You were invited, too.''

''I was? Oh, that's so nice that they wanted me to be with you there for such an important celebration.'' Delight filled her. How wonderful for his friends.

''I'll explain on Monday where you are.''

Where I'll be? Her stomach rolled. *I won't be here,* she realized suddenly. ''Tell them—tell them I'm thrilled for them.'' Not your life, not your friends, she reminded herself. Why was she having such a hard time remembering that?

After rummaging among discarded cartons at the back of a grocery store, Alex and Gillian stacked them in the back seat of his SUV, then drove home. Beside him on the passenger's side, Gillian bent forward, switched on a CD of bluesy saxophone music. It wailed out an old standard, a slow and sultry song about being misty and in love. "I don't think we've ever been this quiet around each other before," she said suddenly.

"What were you thinking about?" He'd been wondering what she would say if he told her what he felt for her. He'd been wondering if he would lose her completely. "Promise me," she'd said. "Don't expect too much." She'd meant a commitment. She'd meant a lifetime together. He had to let her go.

"That was what I was wondering."

"Too late." He leveled a steady stare at her. Despite the darkness in the car, he could read that her thoughts were troubled. "I asked first."

She sighed softly, stared out the window when he braked for a red light. "I keep thinking about Carly. If I'm nervous about the meeting this weekend, I can imagine what she feels."

Alex lowered the volume on the music. "Why are you?"

"I want Rachel and Sean to like her." She turned a concerned expression on him. "I don't know her well, but I feel this connection. Does that sound strange?''

So this was about distress for a woman she was trying hard to link with. He shrugged. Who was he to ask? He'd been an only child. ''Because she's your twin?''

Uncertainty settled on her face. ''I'm not sure. But from what she said, she traveled a lot. And like me she likes Mexican food and spooky movies.''

He thought she sounded pleased with that discovery.

In a slow, lazy move, she stretched on the seat beside him. ''Do you think we have enough boxes?'' she asked, changing subjects suddenly.

Guessing she was looking for a distraction, Alex followed her lead. ''I can't believe we've collected so much stuff in months.''

''This is kind of exciting, Alex. Fun. Usually I only have to pack a few suitcases.''

He thought that was amazing. At the curb he braked behind Joe's car. He couldn't live without his boxes of books. ''I know something that's more fun.'' He cupped a hand at the back of her neck and brushed his lips across hers.

On a giggle, she pushed open the door, leaving him gasping for air. ''Later.''

Groaning, Alex slid out to open the back of the SUV. When she joined him with arms out, he began to stack folded cartons on them.

''I still think this is fun,'' she insisted.

''You think that way because you enjoy going new places, meeting new people.''

He looked up to see her rolling her eyes at him.
"You make it sound as if you're a fuddy-duddy re-
cluse with his nose stuck in the books all day." With
a shake of her head, she turned away and started for
the house. "You've traveled."

And he'd hated it. His arms full of boxes, he followed her up the stairs. What was wrong between
them had nothing to do with their feelings about traveling. He wanted to be rooted, yearned for the bind-
ing ties of a mortgage, family and friends. He needed
to get up every morning and know exactly what
would happen. She would grow restless with his life
while she waited for something unexpected and
thrilling to happen.

"Why didn't you come get me? I'd have helped."
The sound of Joe's voice snapped him back to his
surroundings. Holding the back door open for them,
his father went on, "Loretta's making dinner for all
of us," he said when Alex entered.

Alex stopped in midstride and groaned mentally.
It was chaos. As Gillian dropped the cartons to the
kitchen floor, Alex scanned the room. He'd thought
he had control over the move. He'd been wrong. On
the floor were a dozen half-packed cartons. While
he'd been gone, his father had emptied cupboards.
He'd jammed dish towels into the carton with silverware, plastic containers in with pots and pans.
"This is—" Peripherally he caught Gillian's warning look. *A mess,* he thought, but didn't say the
words. He read Gillian's silent message. Joe was trying to help. Be grateful.

"You two can handle this." Gillian breezed toward the door. "I'll help Loretta with dinner."

"She's making steaks," Joe commented to anyone who might be interested.

Gillian was already gone. Determined to make the best of the situation, Alex drifted toward one carton to finish packing it.

"Alex, do you want these pots in the same box with the bread pans and whatever this is?" he questioned, holding up the object in question.

"That's a colander." He grabbed a roll of shipping tape off the table. "Wherever you decide is okay."

"Don't do that," Joe scolded lightly.

Alex paused in stretching the tape along the flaps of the box. "Don't do what?"

His father cleared his throat. "Act like it doesn't matter where I put something."

It seemed minor, trivial to him suddenly. More important was what would he do without a certain woman in his life. "It doesn't," he answered, taping the box.

"Hey?" Joe said to get his attention and peered over the rim of his glasses at him. "Since when don't you care how something is organized?"

He supposed he was acting strange. "I'm not that bad."

Amusement came in a flash to Joe's face. "Sometimes you are."

Alex couldn't block a smile. "Okay. Sometimes I am." Never in his wildest imaginings had he ever thought he'd be standing side by side with his father and talking like friends. *His father.* It felt good, so damn good.

"You're kind of stubborn, too." Joe's eyes twinkled. "Otherwise I figure you wouldn't be letting her leave."

So this was about Gillian. "She has plans."

"She might change them if you asked her to."

Matchmaking? Was his father actually matchmaking? "She doesn't want this life," he said. He figured that pretty much said it all. And he didn't want to argue with him. After so many strained years, he simply wanted to enjoy his father's company.

Revealing who Alex got his stubborn streak from, Joe went on, "I don't believe that. I've seen how she looks at Shelby—at you. Anyone can see you care, and can see the relationship is working."

He was the second person today to say that.

"If you want her in your life, why haven't you told her? You haven't, have you? Don't be dumb. The two, no, the three of you are perfect together."

Perfect together? "No, we're not."

"Can't figure out why you've convinced yourself that it wouldn't work between you and Gillian." Having had his say, he bent over to tape another box.

His question threw Alex. He had to give some credence to Joe's words. They'd sounded too much like what Grant had said. Why had he convinced himself that he and Gillian were wrong for each other? There was no one else he would share a secret with, trusted more. He'd proven that when he'd told her about Shelby.

"Why don't we join the ladies? After dinner I'll come back and do more of this."

Alex didn't need persuading. Time with Gillian was precious now. He followed Joe out of the apartment and down the stairs. In Loretta's kitchen Gillian was sitting at the kitchen table with Shelby in her arms.

Looking up at Gillian, Shelby's eyes widened. "Did the princess wake up?"

"Oh, yes." Gillian kissed her temple and whispered, "And do you know what happened then?"

Alex felt a tug on his heart at the sight of them with their heads close together, at how perfectly Shelby fit in her arms.

"Oh, sure." His daughter's face shone with a smile. "They lived happily ever after."

Alex pulled in a deep breath against the ache settling in his chest. If only life was like a fairy tale.

Chapter Fourteen

Instead of Joe, Gillian returned to the apartment to help with packing. Satiated from dinner, Alex taped one carton, then lounged against the counter to watch her. He was in more of a mood to sit down and hold her than work.

And she noticed. Bent over a box in the living room, she angled a look back at him and frowned. "You're standing around, doing nothing."

No seriousness anymore, he vowed. He wouldn't make their last days together difficult. "Observant, aren't you?"

"What are you doing?"

"Watching you." She was so animated, running a palm down a denim thigh, tucking a strand of hair behind her ear, pausing to grin at a photograph of

Shelby at two years old. He noticed she'd placed several wrapped photographs in the box with books. He didn't give a hoot about that, but she was churning up hormonal juices every time she bent over and denim strained across her backside.

"By your frown, I gather I'm not supposed to pack these in here, am I?"

Briefly he looked at the photographs. "It's all right."

She sent him a you've-got-to-be-kidding look. "Alex, are you feeling okay?"

Joe had questioned him, too. He didn't care where anything was packed. As she bent again and stretched, he wasn't capable of thinking about anything else. "Let's stop for a while."

She straightened and, over her shoulder, sent him a puzzled look. "Stop?"

"Just—" Facing him now, she bent forward. Alex groaned when the scooped neckline of her top offered him an enticing view of the shadowed flesh between her breasts.

"I suppose you want to lock the door, too?"

The humor in her voice came through clearly. Alex dragged his eyes from the hint of lace at the edge of her bra and caught the impish sparkle in her eyes. "You knew exactly what you were doing, didn't you?"

She took a teasing step back. "Did I?"

Game, he took one forward. As she moved to take another, he lunged for her, snaking an arm around her waist. With the sound of her soft laughter floating over him, he fell back to the sofa, pulling her down on top of him.

"What about Shelby?" she mumbled against a corner of his mouth.

Already needy, he kissed her jaw, her throat. "Loretta and Joe are playing games with her."

"Then you're mine for tonight." She caught his face in her hands. "All mine," she said, and stifled his laugh with a kiss.

All hers, always. Craving slammed at him. He needed her kiss like breath. No leisurely kisses. No gentle strokes. They drove each other. As if both of them sensed this moment might be their last, they let raw emotions lead them, yanked at clothes, raced impatient hands over flesh.

For a few more moments she was his, and nothing mattered but her. On a moan, with a shudder, he traveled with her. On a sigh, she clung as if she'd never leave. For a moment, for one more precious moment, they were one.

The evening had been wonderful, the kind meant to make a person forget troubles. Gillian was grateful for the easygoing time with him. She didn't want to think about problems, about tomorrows. But by morning, tension returned. Nervous about the family meeting, she skipped breakfast and managed one cup of coffee. She couldn't eat, so she kept busy, carrying packing boxes to the moving van.

Several of Alex's colleagues and a few male students with bulging muscles arrived at daybreak and helped Alex haul furniture into the small moving

van. By midafternoon, they'd all left with words that
they would return the next morning to help unpack
everything.

While Alex showered, her brother and sister arrived. Tension coiled into a tight knot in Gillian's
stomach. *Awkward* best described the first minutes
between Carly and Sean and Rachel.

"My God," Sean had said more than once after
seeing Carly and how much she and Gillian looked
alike. Since then he'd been stiff, quiet, standing back
from the three women. Light from the window high-
lighted red in his dark-brown hair. Her brother bore
the countenance of Irish nobility with his nicely
shaped dark brows, deep-set green eyes and aristo-
cratic nose. A formidable man, he bore a demanding
air, and standing so straight, he looked his intimi-
dating best.

Unlike him, her nurturing instincts alive, Rachel
had opened her arms to Carly and treated her with
the same mother-hen attention she'd bestowed on
Gillian while she was growing up. "We're so glad
to find you. Gillian told me you were twins, but—"
She looked from one to the other. "It's stunning how
much you look alike. Where have you lived?"

"Everywhere. My mother—" Carly paused, sent
Gillian an uneasy glance. *Our* mother, her eyes said.

But Lenore Selton would never be a mother to her,
Gillian knew.

"She liked to move around a lot," Carly finished.

"You didn't like that?" Rachel questioned.

"At first, but then I wanted to settle down."

Gillian avoided her brother's stare. She guessed

what he was thinking. Her wanderlust streak obviously had come from Lenore.

"How do you make a living in Silver Creek?" Sean asked, joining in on what Gillian was beginning to view as an interrogation.

Her back straight, Carly's discomfort reached her. "I help at a preschool."

Rachel reacted characteristically at the mention of children. "Oh, that's wonderful."

"Rachel loves kids," Gillian said laughingly. "Could you guess?" Gillian was glad the conversation had shifted. They had a lifetime to learn more about Carly. For now, getting to know and trust each other was more important.

"You'll be staying in Silver Creek because of your aunt's illness?" Rachel questioned.

"Yes, I'm—we're all she has. And you're off to Hawaii?" she asked Gillian.

As if acquiescing to an unspoken agreement not to drill Carly with questions, Sean let his sisters take over.

Though obviously nervous, Carly tried her best. "Hawaii sounds like a wonderful place to go."

"That's what I thought." She should be feeling wonderful, Gillian knew. The job in Hawaii was one that she'd been looking forward to for so long.

She listened to Rachel share with Carly a lighthearted moment about Heather, Kane's niece who'd become Rachel's since she married Kane. "And we might have another baby soon." With her announcement, Rachel glanced at Kane. Beaming, he caught her hand in his.

Gillian came to attention. Because of complications years ago, her sister couldn't get pregnant.

"We've begun proceedings to adopt a little boy from Russia," Rachel explained.

"Oh, Rachel." Gillian rushed to her.

Exclamations of joy surrounded them. Sean pumped Kane's hand. Alex patted him on the back. Rachel received hugs. Though appearing uncertain, Carly gave Rachel a tentative one. Quickly Rachel tightened the embrace.

"What wonderful news." Gillian mustered up a smile. She was happy for Rachel and Kane, but—

There it was again. A flash of discontent. A sense of emptiness. A feeling that something was missing in her life.

Peripherally she saw Alex join Sean. He said something that stirred Sean's laugh. He fit in so perfectly. So why did that thought make her feel like crying?

All of them, including Shelby and Joe and Loretta, went to a nearby Italian restaurant for dinner. Over spaghetti and pizza and wine they kept conversation light. Teasing settled on Alex and his propensity for neatness. Goodnaturedly he accepted jibes that he had labeled and color coded his cartons.

Gillian had a good time, and more than once she noticed that Carly was smiling. "We're going to meet at Christmas," she told Alex when they were alone in the apartment after everyone had left. In the other room Shelby was sleeping on a mattress in her bedroom. Joe had decided to stay at Loretta's, preferring a real bed. Lying beside Alex on the king-size mattress, Gillian snuggled closer. "Rachel wanted to make it once a month, but I won't be able to keep flying in from Hawaii."

He was silent for so long that she wasn't sure he'd heard her. "They all tried today."

"I thought so." She was pleased at how well the first meeting had gone between Rachel and Carly.

Facing her in the darkness, he narrowed his eyes as if trying to see what wasn't visible. "Then why the frown?"

"Sean's not bubbling with warmth for Carly."

Lightly he traced her mouth with a finger. "Your brother has never been Mr. Warmth."

"He used to be a lot different before his divorce. Now he's distrustful of all women."

"Carly's a sister."

"She could still touch his heart," Gillian said, understanding his problem had a lot to do with trust. "He won't open it to anyone other than Rachel and me and the kids, of course. But trust takes time."

On a sigh she shared what bothered her most. "And Carly needs us now. All of us. Think how you'd feel around half siblings. You'd be both wary and hopeful. Now that I've found her, I can't let her go. She's a part of me."

"You can't make other people feel what you do."

"I know," she said softly. She stared at the dark, empty closet across the room. Her clothes were still in the one in Joe's room. Every other closet, every cabinet had been emptied. Only she'd dragged her heels about packing.

Gently he brushed back her hair. "I'm going to miss you."

She wanted to hang on to him and not let him go. "You won't find a wet washcloth hanging on the shower faucet anymore," she teased, aware of how often he'd grumbled about finding one after she'd showered.

"I was getting used to that."

She rested her face on his shoulder. "Let's not say goodbye. Don't drive me to the airport."

"Gillian—"

"Please." She suddenly wanted to cling, to cry. "No goodbyes," she said quietly.

At daybreak everyone was awake. With no furniture in the apartment, they all had cereal and cinnamon rolls at Loretta's kitchen table. This would be the last time they'd be together like this. That one thought stayed with Gillian through breakfast.

"Gillian?" Shelby poked a spoon at doughnut-shaped cereal. "Will you help me with my room?"

Wanting to be a part of their happiness, days ago, she'd returned her rental car and had exchanged a morning airplane ticket for a two o'clock flight. "I'd love to."

While Shelby finished eating, she and Alex climbed the stairs. She gathered up her nightgown and robe and waited for him to walk through the apartment to make sure he'd forgotten nothing. Cleaning wasn't necessary. An immaculate man, he'd left the place clean enough for Loretta to rent out immediately. She draped her clothes over her arm. Earlier this morning she'd packed, then had loaded her luggage into Alex's Bronco to take over to the new house until she left for the airport.

With one final scan of the kitchen, he swept an arm toward the door. "Let's go."

For the next few hours, along with friends who'd met them at the house, they hauled cartons and furniture into it. At noon Alex called for pizzas to feed everyone who'd helped.

While they were all in the other rooms, Gillian joined Shelby in her room, and pushed furniture around. The room had a wonderful view of the backyard and woods beyond it. Though her heart felt heavy, for Shelby's sake she never let her smile slip.

"I can put all my dolls there," she said excitedly, pointing to a corner, "and Daddy's going to make shelves for them, and my animals."

"I'll send you another stuffed animal. This time it'll be from Hawaii." With time growing short, Gillian had used her cell phone a few minutes ago and called a taxi service. She wished now she was staying another day, could help Shelby unpack everything. "Would you like that?"

Shelby faced her. Her smile was gone. "I want you." Tears filled her eyes. "Why do you have to go?" She clung to Gillian's waist. "You don't have to."

"Honey, I'll be back." Gillian dropped to her knees and hugged her hard. Unpacking was forgotten. Her heart heavy, she sat on the rug with Shelby in her arms. She couldn't say how long she held her.

But she felt such need to keep the little one close. "Shelby, I'll come back soon," she said, trying to prepare her for a goodbye. Movement at the doorway made her look up.

"Gillian." Joe stepped in. "It's your taxi. I carried your luggage to it."

She didn't want to move, but if she lingered too long, she'd break down. "I love you, sweetie." She pressed a kiss to the top of Shelby's head, then gave her one more hard hug.

"Gillian." Eyes glistening with tears pinned her. "Don't go."

"Honey, I have to leave."

Joe came near. "I don't know where Alex is," he said and held out his arms to his granddaughter. As if sensing no pleading would help, she sought the comfort of his embrace.

One more time, Gillian touched the little girl's silky dark hair. "It's okay," she told Joe. She and Alex had promised each other that there would be no goodbye. She rested her cheek against Joe's. "Bye." Before she lost it, she made herself turn away, rush outside toward the taxi. She opened the door but paused, looked back at the house and saw Shelby standing by the gate. Her mind filled with one thought. *I really don't want to leave.*

Alex had heard the beep of the taxi and had wandered out to the backyard, telling himself he was honoring Gillian's request for no goodbye. Staying there wasn't easy. Every instinct he possessed urged him to go to her. He stood beside one of the huge pines and worked hard to think about anything else.

Behind him, he heard the back door slam.

"She's leaving," Joe announced before he reached his side.

Alex angled a look at his father. "I need to get Shelby's play set from Loretta's yard."

"Did you hear me?" Determined to have his say, Joe pushed conversation his way. "The taxi came."

Alex felt like snapping at him. Did he really think he hadn't heard the beep? "It'll be a good house." He and Shelby and Joe would make a life for themselves here. But would it be a home without Gillian?

"Alex, are you listening to me?" Joe questioned churlishly.

How could he make him understand why he hadn't told her that he loved her? All this time he could have said something, but never had. He hadn't wanted to pressure her, make her feel they would expect anything from her. "I didn't want her to have any regrets. Nicki—"

"She's *not* Nicole," Joe cut in.

"I know that, but—" He closed his mouth. Of course he knew that. Gillian wasn't anything like Nicki. So what was this really about? Not once had Gillian acted as if she thought he led a boring life. In fact, she'd told him he wore a lot of hats. During a quiet moment between them, she'd laughed and had said she thought he was busier than she was. So why did he keep comparing her with Nicki?

He stared out at the cloudy sky. It wasn't a hard

question to answer, he realized. It was much easier to look for a handy excuse than face himself.

"Alex?" Joe's voice demanded his attention.

"I hear you, Dad," he said more sharply than he'd intended. He wasn't annoyed with him, with anyone but himself. This wasn't about Nicole—or Gillian. It was about him. It was about him not being willing to take a chance, to get hurt again. He'd been crushed once by someone he'd loved, so he'd avoided involvement with another woman. He was protecting himself. But from whom? The one woman who'd never hurt him?

"Will you do something?" Joe urged.

He said more, but Alex didn't catch the words. In a swift move he jumped over the gate. Was he too late? He raced toward the front of the house, saw the taxi turning the corner. He was too late. No, dammit, he couldn't be. He'd go to the airport. He'd stop her.

"Daddy!"

For Shelby, and for himself, he had to make Gillian listen. He yanked his keys from his jeans pocket. Breathing heavier, he whipped around. He would scoop up Shelby and jump in his car. On the way to the airport, he would call Joe, tell him where he was going, and— The thought hung unfinished. His heart quickened as he stared at Shelby standing on the driveway with her hand tight in Gillian's.

A second chance. He'd been given a second chance. All he had to do was grab it. Quickly he crossed the grass to them. He didn't know why she was still here, but he had to take the chance and tell her what he felt, even if she said no.

''Daddy.'' Shelby's eyes shone with joy. ''She's staying.''

Staying. Was she? Or had his daughter misunderstood? ''Honey, go find Grandpa. He needs your help.''

''But—''

''Shelby, go find Grandpa,'' he repeated.

Reluctantly she released Gillian's hand, stepped away. She'd gone only a few feet, then looked back.

''Is she right?'' He moved closer, aching to have Gillian in his arms. ''You're not leaving?''

Instead of looking at him, her gaze remained on Shelby. She gave her a reassuring smile. ''No, I'm not.''

Alex searched her eyes for the love and longing he felt for her. ''Was there more you needed to say to Carly before leaving for Hawaii?''

''This doesn't have anything to do with Carly.''

''Then what?'' His throat felt tight. All he wanted to do was touch her, hold her. ''The job? Did you realize that Hawaii isn't so great?'' he said, and winced at how absurd his words sounded.

Her eyes widened slightly, locked on his. ''It isn't?''

As her lips curved, the small smile encouraged him. Do it, tell her what you feel, he prodded himself. How could he let her leave without telling her that he loved her? ''You could find here all the excitement and adventure you could ever want.''

What sounded like a laugh accompanied her words. ''What are you talking about?''

"Excitement," he returned, growing peeved that he had to explain. "I could give it to you."

"Give it? Oh, Alex." Her smile slipped. So did his courage. "You're serious, aren't you?"

His frown intensified. "Yes, I am."

Gillian wondered when two people who'd always been honest with each other had stopped talking. Did he really think she only wanted excitement in her life? *I could give it to you,* he'd said. Her heart thudded harder. Why would he say that if he didn't want her to stay? "I don't need excitement, or adventure. I wasn't leaving to find that."

"You weren't?" Confusion veed his brows. "Were you leaving because I'm such an idiot?" he asked, taking a step closer.

An idiot? She stared in amazement at him. This from a man whose IQ equaled that of two people. Needing contact to assure herself she'd made the right decision, she set her hand on his chest. Beneath her palm she felt the quick, hard beat of his heart. "I was leaving because I haven't been thinking clearly."

Deliberately she'd kept herself free of commitment, avoided lasting relationships. She'd fed herself nonsense about not wanting regrets and wanting to live her life to the fullest. But while holding Shelby, she realized that what she'd really been doing was avoiding getting close with someone.

She knew now that her parents' deaths had devastated her. Everything she'd done had been because she'd been afraid to love too much. So her family had become only two people, Rachel and Sean. But now there was Carly, too. And Edith. And Joe. And mostly her heart belonged to two other people. Alex and Shelby. Even if she'd left, they still had her heart. "Alex, it's hard to explain, but I've been placing demands on myself, demands not to be satisfied whenever I ran into anything that resembled ties and commitment. I've been afraid."

He touched her, his hands cupping her upper arms. In his touch she felt tension. "So have I," he said softly.

"You, have?"

"Yeah." He framed her face with his hands. "But no more. Listen. I love you. I will never love another as much as I love you."

"Neither will I." She felt like crying suddenly. "I love you, too."

All the strain on his face lifted. "For keeps?" he asked. "Not just friends but—"

Softly she laughed. "Friends. Lovers. All of it."

With a slow shake of his head, in a gesture of relief, he leaned closer, then pressed his forehead to hers. "If you stay, you do get all of us, you know," he said as he drew back to look at her.

She wanted to laugh, cry, ached to hug him because he looked so uncharacteristically uncertain. "Us?"

"Me. Shelby, Joe. All of us."

How close she'd come to losing everything, she reflected. "That sounds wonderful."

As if those were the words he'd been waiting for, he tugged her to him and laughed softly against her cheek. "Gillian, I love you. I'm not sure when it started, but I don't want to live without you."

Lightly she pressed a finger to his lips to silence him.

"You won't regret staying," he insisted. "I promise."

"Kiss me," she whispered.

The words came out muffled as his mouth sought hers with a kiss that was so sweet and filled with more love than she thought possible. She had believed she could keep herself free of everyday ties, but her heart was bound to these people. She loved all of them, especially this man.

"Daddy."

And his child. Gillian drew back only enough to watch Shelby dash their way. "I love your daughter, too."

"She loves you," Alex assured her a second before Shelby leaped at him. Holding her, he kissed her cheek. "Do you still want me to ask her that question?"

Shelby's eyes grew wide.

"What question?" Gillian asked as they both grinned at her.

"Do you want to be my mommy?" Shelby said in a rush.

Alex chuckled. "Will you marry us?"

On a laugh Gillian linked her arm with the one Alex had around Shelby and leaned closer to him. "I can't think of anything I'd want to do more."

Epilogue

''How long does it take?''

Rachel laughed and reached over to pat her brother on the shoulder. ''Sean, babies come when they're ready. Look at Alex. Daddy-to-be is calm and steady.''

''Sure he is,'' Kane bantered, lounging in one of the chrome-and-vinyl, turquoise-colored chairs in the hospital waiting room. He shifted a sleeping Heather to his other arm and adjusted the yellow blanket wrapped around her.

''Kane, don't be so hard on him,'' Rachel scolded her husband. ''You were an absolute wreck when we were waiting for Peter to come off the plane.''

''Who would blame me. He was coming all the way from another country,'' he said about the dark-haired, four-year-old they'd adopted. On the floor near Kane, Peter stacked several colored blocks that Rachel had dumped from a small tote bag a few minutes earlier.

Alex stopped pacing and sat back on a window ledge in the huge beige-colored room. As much as he appreciated everyone showing up, and all the words of encouragement and support, he wanted to be in the other room with his wife. The nurse said she'd call him as soon as they had Gillian ready.

"Daddy?"

He focused on Shelby standing beside him now. Alex slipped an arm around her small waist. She'd been as excited as he and Gillian and Joe about Gillian's pregnancy. All she wanted was to be a big sister. "What do you want, honey?" he asked, knowing he'd give her anything she wanted at the moment.

She pointed to the vending machine. "Can I get a candy bar over there?"

"I'll take her," Sean volunteered.

Kane stood with Heather. "We want something, too." The toddler in his arms slept without a care for anything else.

"Heather wants one?" Rachel teased.

"I'm getting one for you," he told his wife. "You're the one with the sweet tooth."

Alex's attention shifted to the nurse coming down the hall.

"Mr. Hunter? You can join your wife. It won't be long now. I understand you're her coach."

Lord, he hoped he remembered everything. "Right."

''Give her our love,'' Rachel called out.

On the way he paused by Shelby and kissed her cheek, then sprinted down the hall to Gillian's room.

She looked lovelier than he'd ever seen her, he decided the moment he reached the doorway of her room and saw her smile. Quickly he moved to her side, took her hand.

''We've been timing the contractions,'' the nurse informed him. ''We're doing fine.''

''What's with the 'we' stuff,'' he whispered to Gillian.

She laughed, then winced as a contraction hit. ''Don't do that,'' she scolded.

''What?'' he asked, hating the pain he was seeing in her face.

''Make me laugh. This is—whoa.'' Panting, she tightened her fingers harder on his hand. Then groaned. ''Get ready, Daddy. Here comes your son.''

He was beautiful. Gillian couldn't take her eyes off the baby in her arms. Beaming with pride, she nestled her son in her arms closer to her breast while the doctor and nurses left.

Sitting on the bed beside her now, Alex ran a gentle hand over the top of his son's reddish hair. ''Thank you.'' He leaned forward and kissed Gillian. ''Thank you, sweetheart.''

''Can we come in?'' Rachel asked from the doorway.

''Oh, Daddy.'' Shelby rushed to the bed.

For the next few moments everyone took their turn oohing and aahing over the baby. Shelby kept touching her brother's soft hair. Sean decided the baby looked like a Quinn.

Rachel thought the baby had Alex's features. "And he's so beautiful," she gushed.

She glows with happiness all the time since she's been with Kane, Gillian decided. "He is, isn't he?"

"Hi, am I too late," a voice called out from the doorway.

"Oh, Carly." Gillian held out an arm to her, urging her to come near for a hug.

"You missed Alex sweating," Kane teased.

Carly smiled along with the rest, then came to Gillian.

"I'm so glad you got here," Gillian told her.

Rachel leaned closer over Gillian's bed. "All that hair. And a cleft in his chin."

As Joe came in, Kane gestured with an arm toward him. "The baby looks like his grandpa."

Standing nearby, craning his neck to get a better look at the baby, Joe beamed.

"What do you think, Dad?" Alex asked.

"I think he's fortunate. He looks like his mother," Joe quipped.

Gillian laughed, looked around her at her family, at the smiles, listened to the laughter. And in the middle of them all was Carly, where she belonged, with family. "I'm so happy," she said to Alex as he took a seat beside her again and curled his hand around hers.

"So am I." He bent forward to kiss her. She might not have needed any more excitement in her life. But she'd sure brought a lot of it into his. "Thank you."

He kissed her again. Never had he expected this kind of happiness. And he had it all because of her. She was still his best friend. And his love. His life.

* * * * *

Beloved author
Sherryl Woods
is back with a brand-new miniseries

THE CALAMITY JANES

**Five women. Five Dreams.
A lifetime of friendship....**

On Sale May 2001—DO YOU TAKE THIS REBEL?
Silhouette Special Edition

On Sale August 2001—COURTING THE ENEMY
Silhouette Special Edition

On Sale September 2001—TO CATCH A THIEF
Silhouette Special Edition

On Sale October 2001—THE CALAMITY JANES
Silhouette Single Title

On Sale November 2001—WRANGLING THE REDHEAD
Silhouette Special Edition

"Sherryl Woods is an author who writes with
a very special warmth, wit, charm and intelligence."
—*New York Times* bestselling author
Heather Graham Pozzessere

Available at your favorite retail outlet.

Where love comes alive™

Visit Silhouette at www.eHarlequin.com   SSETCJR

If you enjoyed what you just read,
then we've got an offer you can't resist!

Take 2 bestselling love stories FREE!

Plus get a FREE surprise gift!

Clip this page and mail it to Silhouette Reader Service™

IN U.S.A.	IN CANADA
3010 Walden Ave.	P.O. Box 609
P.O. Box 1867	Fort Erie, Ontario
Buffalo, N.Y. 14240-1867	L2A 5X3

YES! Please send me 2 free Silhouette Special Edition® novels and my free surprise gift. After receiving them, if I don't wish to receive anymore, I can return the shipping statement marked cancel. If I don't cancel, I will receive 6 brand-new novels every month, before they're available in stores! In the U.S.A., bill me at the bargain price of $3.80 plus 25¢ shipping and handling per book and applicable sales tax, if any*. In Canada, bill me at the bargain price of $4.21 plus 25¢ shipping and handling per book and applicable taxes**. That's the complete price and a savings of at least 10% off the cover prices—what a great deal! I understand that accepting the 2 free books and gift places me under no obligation ever to buy any books. I can always return a shipment and cancel at any time. Even if I never buy another book from Silhouette, the 2 free books and gift are mine to keep forever.

235 SEN DFNN
335 SEN DFNP

Name	(PLEASE PRINT)	
Address	Apt.#	
City	State/Prov.	Zip/Postal Code

* Terms and prices subject to change without notice. Sales tax applicable in N.Y.
** Canadian residents will be charged applicable provincial taxes and GST.
   All orders subject to approval. Offer limited to one per household and not valid to
   current Silhouette Special Edition® subscribers.
® are registered trademarks of Harlequin Enterprises Limited.

SPED01
©1998 Harlequin Enterprises Limited

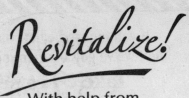

Feel like a star with Silhouette.

We will fly you and a guest to New York City for an exciting weekend stay at a glamorous 5-star hotel. Experience a refreshing day at one of New York's trendiest spas and have your photo taken by a professional. Plus, receive $1,000 U.S. spending money!

Flowers...long walks...dinner for two... how does Silhouette Books make romance come alive for you?

Send us a script, with 500 words or less, along with visuals (only drawings, magazine cutouts or photographs or combination thereof). Show us how Silhouette Makes Your Love Come Alive. Be creative and have fun. No purchase necessary. All entries must be clearly marked with your name, address and telephone number. All entries will become property of Silhouette and are not returnable. **Contest closes September 28, 2001.**

Please send your entry to: **Silhouette Makes You a Star!**

In U.S.A.
P.O. Box 9069
Buffalo, NY, 14269-9069

In Canada
P.O. Box 637
Fort Erie, ON, L2A 5X3

Look for contest details on the next page, by visiting www.eHarlequin.com or request a copy by sending a self-addressed envelope to the applicable address above. Contest open to Canadian and U.S. residents who are 18 or over. Void where prohibited.

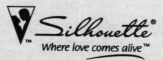

Our lucky winner's photo will appear in a Silhouette ad. Join the fun!

SRMYAS1

HARLEQUIN "SILHOUETTE MAKES YOU A STAR!" CONTEST 1308
OFFICIAL RULES
NO PURCHASE NECESSARY TO ENTER

1. To enter, follow directions published in the offer to which you are responding. Contest begins June 1, 2001, and ends on September 28, 2001. Entries must be postmarked by September 28, 2001, and received by October 5, 2001. Enter by hand-printing (or typing) on an 8 ½" x 11" piece of paper your name, address (including zip code), contest number/name and attaching a script containing <u>500 words</u> or less, <u>along with drawings, photographs or magazine cutouts, or combinations thereof</u> (i.e., collage) <u>on no larger than 9" x 12"</u> piece of paper, describing how the <u>Silhouette books make romance come alive for you.</u> Mail via first-class mail to: Harlequin "Silhouette Makes You a Star!" Contest 1308, (in the U.S.) P.O. Box 9069, Buffalo, NY 14269-9069, (in Canada) P.O. Box 637, Fort Erie, Ontario, Canada L2A 5X3. Limit one entry per person, household or organization.

2. Contests will be judged by a panel of members of the Harlequin editorial, marketing and public relations staff. Fifty percent of criteria will be judged against script and fifty percent will be judged against drawing, photographs and/or magazine cutouts. Judging criteria will be based on the following:

   - Sincerity—25%
   - Originality and Creativity—50%
   - Emotionally Compelling—25%

   In the event of a tie, duplicate prizes will be awarded. Decisions of the judges are final.

3. All entries become the property of Torstar Corp. and may be used for future promotional purposes. Entries will not be returned. No responsibility is assumed for lost, late, illegible, incomplete, inaccurate, nondelivered or misdirected mail.

4. Contest open only to residents of the U.S. (<u>except Puerto Rico</u>) and Canada who are 18 years of age or older, and is void wherever prohibited by law; all applicable laws and regulations apply. Any litigation within the Province of Quebec respecting the conduct or organization of a publicity contest may be submitted to the Régie des alcools, des courses et des jeux for a ruling. Any litigation respecting the awarding of a prize may be submitted to the Régie des alcools, des courses et des jeux only for the purpose of helping the parties reach a settlement. Employees and immediate family members of Torstar Corp. and D. L. Blair, Inc., their affiliates, subsidiaries and all other agencies, entities and persons connected with the use, marketing or conduct of this contest are not eligible to enter. Taxes on prizes are the sole responsibility of the winner. Acceptance of any prize offered constitutes permission to use winner's name, photograph or other likeness for the purposes of advertising, trade and promotion on behalf of Torstar Corp., its affiliates and subsidiaries without further compensation to the winner, unless prohibited by law.

5. Winner will be determined no later than November 30, 2001, and will be notified by mail. Winner will be required to sign and return an Affidavit of Eligibility/Release of Liability/Publicity Release form within 15 days after winner notification. Noncompliance within that time period may result in disqualification and an alternative winner may be selected. All travelers must execute a Release of Liability prior to ticketing and must possess required travel documents (e.g., passport, photo ID) where applicable. Trip must be booked by December 31, 2001, and completed within one year of notification. No substitution of prize permitted by winner. Torstar Corp. and D. L. Blair, Inc., their parents, affiliates and subsidiaries are not responsible for errors in printing of contest, entries and/or game pieces. In the event of printing or other errors that may result in unintended prize values or duplication of prizes, all affected game pieces or entries shall be null and void. **Purchase or acceptance of a product offer does not improve your chances of winning.**

6. Prizes: (1) Grand Prize—A 2-night/3-day trip for two (2) to New York City, including round-trip coach air transportation nearest winner's home and hotel accommodations (double occupancy) at The Plaza Hotel, a glamorous afternoon makeover at <u>a trendy New York spa,</u> $1,000 in U.S. spending money and an opportunity to <u>have a professional photo taken and appear in a Silhouette advertisement</u> (approximate retail value: $7,000). (10) Ten Runner-Up Prizes of gift packages (retail value $50 ea.). Prizes consist of only those items listed as part of the prize. Limit one prize per person. Prize is valued in U.S. currency.

7. For the name of the winner (available after December 31, 2001) send a self-addressed, stamped envelope to: Harlequin "Silhouette Makes You a Star!" Contest 1197 Winners, P.O. Box 4200 Blair, NE 68009-4200 or you may access the www.eHarlequin.com Web site through February 28, 2002.

Contest sponsored by Torstar Corp., P.O Box 9042, Buffalo, NY 14269-9042.

In September 2001,

Silhouette

SPECIAL EDITION™
presents the final book in

DIANA PALMER's

exciting new *Soldiers of Fortune* trilogy:

THE
LAST MERCENARY
(SE #1417)

Traveling far and wide to rescue Callie Kirby from a dangerous
desperado was far less daunting for Micah Steele than trying to
combat his potent desire for the virginal beauty. For the heavenly
taste of Callie's sweetly tempting lips was slowly driving Micah
insane. Was the last mercenary *finally* ready to claim his bride?

Don't miss any of the adventurous
SOLDIERS OF FORTUNE *tales from*
international bestselling author Diana Palmer!

MERCENARY'S WOMAN, SR #1444
THE WINTER SOLDIER, SD #1351
THE LAST MERCENARY, SE #1417

Soldiers of Fortune...prisoners of love.

Available only from Silhouette Books at your favorite retail outlet.

Silhouette®
Where love comes alive™

Visit Silhouette at www.eHarlequin.com

SSELM

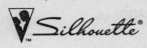

COMING NEXT MONTH

#1417 THE LAST MERCENARY—Diana Palmer
Soldiers of Fortune
Mercenary Micah Steele hadn't seen his stepsister, Callie Kirby, since their forbidden attraction led to a family split. Now kidnapped by a drug lord, Callie was the bait to reel Micah in—and he came running. But when the adventure was over, would the last mercenary finally claim his bride?

#1418 TO CATCH A THIEF—Sherryl Woods
The Calamity Janes
When Gina Petrillo returned to Winding River for her high school reunion, trouble followed her home in the form of lawyer Rafe O'Donnell. He was sure that Gina had stolen money from his clients. But once he caught his "thief," would the only thing she really had stolen turn out to be his heart?

#1419 WHEN I DREAM OF YOU—Laurie Paige
The Windraven Legacy
The Windoms and Herriots were archenemies for three generations—until Megan Windom met Kyle Herriot and hate turned into passion. But when their investigation revealed the meaning behind Megan's nightmares, they knew their only chance for a future…was to resolve the past.

#1420 ANOTHER MAN'S CHILDREN—Christine Flynn
While Lauren Edwards baby-sat her brother's toddlers, his business partner, Zach McKendrick, stopped by to lend a hand—and wound up lending a little more than that. But a past love and a plane crash had left Zach scarred inside and out. Would this ex-test pilot realize that Lauren's love could heal all wounds?

#1421 HER SECRET AFFAIR—Arlene James
Interior designer Chey Simmons was hired to restore Brodie Todd's crumbling mansion, not his heart. But when he needed help exposing deceptive family members, Chey pretended to be his lover. Would her secret affair soon become a public proposal?

#1422 AN ABUNDANCE OF BABIES—Marie Ferrarella
The Baby of the Month Club
After years of separation Stephanie Yarbourough encountered past love Dr. Sebastian Caine while he delivered her babies—twins! Now, if she would only put her faith in Sebastian once more, double the babies could have double the love.